FOREVER SAVAGE

MAYHEM MAKERS

ANDI RHODES

Blue Journey Publishing

Copyright © 2023 by Andi Rhodes

All rights reserved.

No part of this book may be reproduced in any form or by any electronic or mechanical means, including information storage and retrieval systems, without written permission from the author, except for the use of brief quotations in a book review.

Cover Artwork - © Clarise Tan @ CT Cover Creations

Edited by Darcie Fisher.

This is for all the girls who don't believe in love. I'm here to tell you that it exists. The problem is it doesn't always present itself in fairytale form. Sometimes, if you're lucky, it's so much better than any bedtime story your mother ever read to you when you were a little girl.

ALSO BY ANDI RHODES

Broken Rebel Brotherhood

Broken Souls

Broken Innocence

Broken Boundaries

Broken Rebel Brotherhood: Complete Series Box set

Broken Rebel Brotherhood: Next Generation

Broken Hearts

Broken Wings

Broken Mind

Bastards and Badges

Stark Revenge

Slade's Fall

Jett's Guard

Soulless Kings MC

Fender

Joker

Piston

Greaser

Riker

Trainwreck

Squirrel

Gibson

Flash

Royal

Satan's Legacy MC

Snow's Angel

Toga's Demons

Magic's Torment

Duck's Salvation

Dip's Flame

Devil's Handmaidens MC

Harlow's Gamble

Peppermint's Twist

Mama's Rules

Valhalla Rising MC

Viking

Mayhem Makers

Forever Savage

Saints Purgatory MC

Unholy Soul

DISCLAIMER:

Motorcycles, Mobsters, and Mayhem (MMM) is a real event; however, Forever Savage is a work of fiction. While MMM is mentioned in Lead and Nova's story, Forever Savage does not represent anything that actually takes place at MMM. The events in this story are entirely fictional and products of the author's imagination.

Lead...

Everyone has a dark side, a part of them that they try to keep hidden. As President of the Black Savages MC, my darkness is a constant companion, one I embrace with open arms. But even I have limits.

Sticking your nose where it doesn't belong isn't without consequences. And mine come in the form of a feisty author who makes me want to step into the light. Neither of us believe in fairytales, but something about her has me vowing to be the knight in leather armor who shows her what it's like to be forever savage.

Nova...

Growing up, I lived for the fairy tales my mother would read to me at bedtime. As I got older, I learned that fairy tales are for fools.

As a motorcycle club romance author, I often wonder what it would be like to have my biker heroes step off the page and save me from my villain. But when fiction collides with reality, I'm not prepared. I want my knight on a chrome horse more than anything, but can I embrace the darkness I keep hidden? Can I become forever savage?

PROLOGUE

Nova

Six years old...

"And they lived happily ever after."

I smile up at Mommy and squeeze my teddy bear. She reads me a bedtime story every night, and they're always fairy tales. I love fairy tales.

"Time to get some sleep, princess." Mommy's smile is so big, but she looks tired. She got home late from work, so maybe that's it.

"Read me one more?" I ask, as I do every night.

"Not tonight." She tries to hide her yawn behind her hand, but when I giggle, she knows she's been caught. She leans in close and tickles me. "Sleep, princess. I'll read two books tomorrow."

"Promise?" Mommy never breaks a promise.

"Promise."

She stands and crosses to the door.

"Mommy?" I stop her from turning off the light.

"Yeah, princess?"

"Is Daddy Prince Charming?"

"Well, no. There's only one Prince Charming and that's the one in the story. But Daddy *is* a prince."

"He is?"

"He sure is. Daddy's *my* prince. And there are lots of other princes out there for all the princesses."

"Hey, I'm a princess! You call me that. You call me princess."

"You're the prettiest princess of them all."

"So there's a prince somewhere for me?"

"Absolutely. Someday, when you're all grown up, you're gonna meet a wonderful prince who will sweep you off your feet. You'll fall in love with him like I did with Daddy, and you'll live happily ever after."

"Wow."

Mommy chuckles. "Sleep, Novalyn. It's now past your bedtime." She turns the light off. "Love you."

I roll over with my teddy bear and snuggle into the covers. "G'night, Mommy. Love you too."

When I fall asleep, I dream about my very own grown-up fairytale, completely oblivious to the fact that, as I age, life will change, love will die, and fairy tales will cease to exist.

Chapter One
NOVA
Present day...

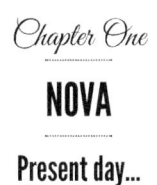

"You can't miss my wedding."

Rolling my eyes, I tuck my cell tighter between my ear and shoulder while I scoop some mac n' cheese into my bowl. This is my mom's fourth marriage. After she caught my dad cheating with his secretary—could he be a bigger cliché?—Mom changed. Hell, we both did. But while I closed my heart to love, she spread her legs for lust. Harsh? Probably. True? Totally.

"Mom, I told you months ago that I had this signing," I remind her.

I carry my lunch to my desk and flop into my office chair.

"Novalyn, I think my wedding trumps your little book signing. Besides, I really want you to meet..."

Mom goes on and on about her latest husband-to-be, and I tune her out while I eat. It's not often I have time for lunch, and I refuse to let a phone call from her ruin this for me. Mom stops talking just as I'm swallowing the last of my food.

"Can't you reschedule the ceremony?" I ask, pretending like I heard the last ten minutes of her babbling and actually give a damn. Don't get me wrong, I love my mom, but how many times does she expect me to stand by her side and smile while she throws her life away?

Three, apparently.

Okay, to be fair, marriages two and three only lasted a few months each, so it's not the rest of her life she's tossing in the dumpster, but still.

"When did you become so selfish?" Mom snaps. "I raised you better than that."

"You also raised me to believe in fairy tales. And look where that got us."

"You have your father to thank for that," she scoffs. "How is he by the way? Still sleeping with what's her name?"

"If you wanna know how Dad is, ask him."

"You know I don't care how he's doing."

"Then why—"

"The ceremony will be at one, but I need you to be at the hotel at seven that morning. Better yet, come the night before. That way you can handle any last—."

"Gotta go, Mom," I sing-song as I lower the phone. "Darcie's calling for our weekly meeting. Love you."

I disconnect the call and toss my cell on my desk. Leaning back, I kick my feet up and rub my temples to ease the migraine forming. I close my eyes and take a few deep breaths. I must doze off because the next thing I know, I'm flailing as my phone rings.

"What?" I snap after answering.

"Uh, hello to you too," Darcie, my assistant, says.

"Sorry." I sigh. "I fell asleep at my desk."

"Aw, hell. Who's Dee marrying now?"

I chuckle. "How'd you know?"

"I've been your best friend since we were fourteen. And the only time you fall asleep in the middle of the day is if you have a migraine. *And*," she says with exaggeration. "Your mother is the only trigger you have for migraines."

"I have no clue what his name is," I admit. "I tuned out most of what she had to say after she told me her wedding is more important than my career."

Darcie whistles. "I think you've proven that being an author isn't a passing fancy. Fuck, you've got twenty-two books out and you just bought a house. What more does she want from you?"

"She wants me to skip the Motorcycles, Mobsters, and Mayhem Author Event in Texas because, get this..." I take a deep breath. "She scheduled her wedding on the same day."

Darcie groans.

"I know, right?"

"Ah, well..."

I know that tone. Darcie only uses that tone when there's something she doesn't want to tell me. My stomach sinks.

"What?"

"God, Nova, I hate this. But..."

"You can't go, can you?"

"I'm sorry," she rushes to say. "So fucking sorry. But my boss won't give me the time off."

"I'm your boss," I whine, knowing I sound like a child.

"You are," she agrees. "But it's my job at the Country Club that pays the bills."

Darcie only acts as my assistant ten hours a week, unless I've got a book release or signing event. And she's insanely efficient so she gets more marketing and administrative work done in those ten hours than I would in two weeks.

"Ugh, fine."

"You know if there was any way around it, I'd take it. Unfortunately, no one can cover my shifts."

"It's okay, Dar. I know you'd go if you could."

"Uh, yeah. I was looking forward to fangirling. Do you have any idea how many authors I wanted to meet?"

"I do," I say with a chuckle. "You've made a point to tell me almost every single day."

"I don't know what you're talking about."

"Keep telling yours—"

"Nova!"

I groan at Rodney's shout. My boyfriend doesn't live with me, but he does have a key since he's here more than at his own place.

"In my office," I call back. "Gotta go, Dar. Rod's here."

"Talk to ya later."

"You know it."

I disconnect the call just as Rodney walks into the room.

"Who was that?" he asks.

"Darcie. She was calling to let me know she can't go to Texas."

"Oh." He sits on the couch across from my desk and kicks his feet up onto the coffee table. I open my mouth to remind him that I hate when he does that, but he doesn't let me get a word out. "I'll go with you."

I sit a little straighter. "What?"

Rod shrugs. "You need an assistant, and I'm free." What he doesn't say is he's free because he still isn't working. He was fired from his last job because he punched his boss. Same with the job before that. "Besides, you know I don't like you going on these vacations without me."

I resist the urge to roll my eyes. As much as I want to, I know it would only result in a fight. What I can't ignore is the fact that he has no respect for my work.

"It's not a vacation," I tell him. "It's work."

"You're going to a resort in Texas for a book signing. There will be cover models there," he argues. "Doesn't exactly seem like work."

"Just because I love what I do doesn't mean it's—" I press my lips together and inhale. No good will come from having this conversation for what has to be the millionth time. "Ya know what? Never mind."

"It's settled then. I'm coming with you."

I rack my brain for an alternative, but the signing is in a week and a half. There's no time to find someone else, *anyone* else, to go.

Fuck.

"If that's what you want," I say, resignation thickening my tone.

Rod laughs as he stands. "It's what I want." He walks to the door before turning back to face me and leaning against the door frame. "So, what's for dinner?"

"Don't know." I tip my head toward my computer. "I've got work to do."

"In other words, pizza… again."

"You know I've got a deadline," I remind him.

"How is that my problem?"

I sigh. "It's not, Rod. But I don't have time to cook, so it's either takeout or you make something."

Rod straightens and crosses his arms over his chest. "Or we could go out to eat."

"Do you really expect me to forget about my deadline because you don't want pizza or can't be bothered to cook?"

"I expect you to spend time with me when I come over," he snaps. "Work for a few hours, but then we're going out." He turns and leaves, but shouts from the hallway. "You've got boxes of shit on the porch."

And you can't be bothered to carry them in.

Excitement mixes with annoyance. I know what's in those boxes, and it isn't shit. Rod's *demands* forgotten, I race to the front door and yank it open with a squeal. I love delivery day, especially when the deliveries are full of books and swag.

It takes me fifteen minutes to lug all the boxes inside and

to my office, and the entire time I'm doing that, Rod is sitting on the couch with the TV blaring some show about cars.

Once I get everything situated, I force myself to focus on writing. I push thoughts of my mom, Darcie, and Rodney from my mind and get lost in the world of Harleys and alpha heroes.

Chapter Two
LEAD

"I could eat a fucking horse, Prez."

I lean back in the booth and grin at Arrow, the Vice President of Black Savages MC. We've been riding all day to get home, but decided to stop and eat at the diner that sits at the edge of town. Normally, we'd be dying to get to the clubhouse, but hunger won out this time.

"That's new. Usually, you're all about the pussy after a long run."

"Bro, I can't have my stomach growling while I'm goin' down on a bitch," he counters. "Kills the mood."

"And here I thought your sparkling personality is what kept the ladies happy," Mercenary, our Enforcer, adds.

"Fuck off," Arrow barks, with laughter in his tone. "Chicks love me."

"They love your monster cock," Brew gripes. "Shit, fuck *eating* horses. You're hung like one."

"And here I thought y'all would be normal today."

I smile up at the waitress. "We are normal, Kit."

"On what planet?"

Kit shakes her head with a chuckle. "You guys always make my day when you come in."

"I could make your night too," Arrow teases with a bob of his brows.

She taps her pen on her chin as if considering his proposition. "Hung like a horse, huh?"

"Aw, darlin', you'll just have to ride me and find out."

She stares a moment longer before scribbling something on her order pad. After tearing off the top page, she slides it across the table to Arrow. "I'm off at eleven." Her smile widens as she shifts into full-on waitress mode. "So, what can I get y'all? The special tonight is the meatloaf."

We each give her our orders, and when she walks away, Mercenary glares at Arrow. "You've gotta pick up chicks everywhere you go, don't you? Like it's a compulsion or some shit."

"I can't help it if women love me."

"They love your cock," Brew says bitterly. "*You* they could do without."

"Hey, bro, it's your fault that just happened," Arrow bites out. "Why do you know how big my dick is anyway?"

"Because you've always got it hangin' out," Brew snaps. "And because I'm the unlucky bastard that usually gets stuck sharing a room with you on overnight runs." He shudders as if disgusted and focuses on me. "I've seen things I can't unsee, Prez. Disturbing things."

"You're all idiots," I say.

"When the club gets a bill for my therapy, you'll know why," Brew tells me. "Very disturbing things, Prez."

"I don't doubt it. But the club ain't paying for no therapy. That's what our Harleys are for."

"No amount of riding will scrub my brain clean."

"A head shrinker won't either," Mercenary says.

"We're gonna be eating in a few minutes so can we cut the cock talk? I don't need the mental images," I snap.

"That's what I've been… "

Two customers enter the diner, and I miss the rest of what Brew says. The diner is full of people, but they all disappear as I focus on the newcomers. It's as if I'm traveling through a wind tunnel and nothing but getting to the end of it matters.

Holy fucking shit.

Silently praying that the man is the woman's brother, I let my gaze wander from her face to her slender neck, and then it moves further south to the tits filling out a golden yellow tee and lower still to the way her dark-wash jeans mold to her curves like a second skin. Her jet-black hair is cut just below her shoulders, and her eyes are a seafoam green.

She scans the diner, and her eyes hesitate on me, but the man grabs her arm and practically drags her behind him to a table. My inner beast snaps and snarls at the action.

"Lead!"

Sights and sounds penetrate the wind tunnel, and I slowly turn to look at Mercenary. "What?"

"What the fuck was that, man?"

"What was what?"

"You just growled like a fucking rabid dog or some shit."

I guess the beast broke through a bit.

"Whatever fucker," I bite out and return my attention to the woman.

The man slings his arm over her shoulder—so not brother and sister—and whispers something in her ear. She opens her mouth to speak but is interrupted when Kit steps up to their booth to take their orders.

The woman doesn't look at all happy to be here. The smile she gives Kit is fake as fuck, but the man doesn't seem to notice, or care. When he gives his order to Kit, it's clear by his grin and the way he leans toward her that he's flirting shamelessly.

"Order up!" the cook calls just as he dings the bell that sits on the pass-through.

Kit finishes with the couple and rushes to grab the full plates of food. As she carries them to our table, her eyes dart around the diner as if assessing what her next task will be. It's what makes her a great waitress. She's always anticipating what the customers want.

"Here you go," Kit says as she sets the plates in front of us. "Enjoy guys."

I snake my arm out and grab her wrist. "What's their deal?" I ask as I tip my head at the couple.

Kit glances over her shoulder and when she returns her attention to me, she's sporting a frown, which is something I've never seen on her.

"That would be Rod and Nova." She rolls her eyes dramatically. "Guy's a prick. Always flirts with me in front of her, but if she so much as looks in the direction of a male customer, he gets pissed."

"Do they come in here a lot?"

"What do you care?" Arrow asks around a mouthful of mashed potatoes.

"I've just never seen them before," I say with a tone that I hope conveys how much I *don't* care. "I like to know who's in my fucking town, that's all."

"He's in here at least once a week," Kit says. "Nova comes in a lot, but not always with him. Mostly she's here late at night with her laptop, hard at work. Says the pie helps her concentrate."

"Huh."

Arrow swallows another bite of food and looks over his shoulder at the pair. When he turns back around, his eyes are narrowed. "I know that guy." He points his fork at me. "And you do too."

"Ah, nope, don't think so."

"Bro, look closer."

Brew now looks over his shoulder to see what all the fuss is about, and Mercenary stares.

"Yeah, you know him," our Enforcer says.

"Aw, fuck," Brew mumbles when he's facing me again. "He's on our list."

"Uh, I don't think I wanna hear this," Kit says. "Can I get y'all anything else?"

"Nah, we're good, Kit," Arrow says. "Thanks."

"Don't lose my number," she tells him with a wink and then walks away to take care of other diners.

"I don't know about you jagoffs, but I'm getting laid tonight," Arrow taunts.

"Why's he on our list?" I ask, not giving a damn about Arrow's sexual conquests and needing to bring the conversation back to business.

Brew shakes his head as if annoyed. "Prez, why the hell do people make it to our list? They either owe us money, hurt someone we care about, or wronged the club in some way." He lifts a finger for each reason.

"That doesn't exactly narrow it down," I grit.

Arrow heaves a sigh. "He owes us money." He shoves another bite of mashed potatoes in his mouth but doesn't stop talking. "Well, not us specifically, but his dealer. Dude's got a fucking temper and can't keep a job, so he can't afford his habit. But that doesn't seem to matter."

"And the dealer's putting up with it?"

"Yeah, he's on our list too," Brew says. "But we take care of him tomorrow, so Rod's source will be cut off, and he'll have to answer to us."

As our Road Captain, Brew is integral to the coordination and planning of taking out our enemies. Between him,

Mercenary, and Arrow, the list is never too long, but it's not as short as I'd like.

"Can we move past dickwad there," Arrow begins as he tips his head back to indicate Rod and Nova. "C'mon guys, I'm gettin' laid tonight. We should be celebrating."

"Eat your damn food," I snap.

We all dig into our meals, but even as I eat, I can't stop stealing glances at Nova. Every once in a while I catch her staring at me, but when I do she quickly averts her gaze and returns to absently nodding at Rod.

Rod... I rack my brain for any memory of him, but despite what my brothers say, I've got nothing. When we vote on who goes on the list, I hear a name and that's it. It isn't often I know what the people look like or that I go on the runs to handle them.

Last night's run was different. The target was different. And he's now shark bait off the coast of Washington, so his transgressions have been punished. His victim won't ever forget, but I refuse to let him take up space in my head any longer. The moment I shoved his corpse off the cliff, I forgot about him.

That's how I survive this life. A whole lot of bad wrapped up in a fuck ton of forget.

"I want in on that run," I say to Arrow when I'm done eating.

He arches a brow. "Why?"

"Does it matter?"

Arrow shrugs. "Guess not."

"Any clue when it's gonna happen?"

"In the next week or so," Mercenary says.

"Just make sure to tell me when and where," I order.

"You got it, Prez."

As the three of them order and eat their dessert, I keep

my attention on Rod and Nova. A week. I can wait a week. Right?

And then what?

And then... who fucking knows? Maybe the sexy Nova will need a shoulder to cry on.

Chapter Three

NOVA

Eight days later...

"There's no way you need all this shit."

I roll my suitcase out of the bedroom and down the hall to the living room, leaving Rod to follow if he wants. We're leaving for Texas tonight, so I'm trying to get the car packed and, as usual, my boyfriend is not making himself useful.

"Nova, stop," he shouts as he grabs my arm and spins me around.

"What?" I ask with exaggerated patience.

"We're not *moving* to Texas. Why the hell do you need all this?"

Crossing my arms over my chest, I glare at him. "What exactly is it that you think I don't need, Rod?"

Not only will we be in Texas for three days, but we'll also be making several stops on the trip down and back. The drive itself is gonna take three days each way. I don't know how much less he expects me to pack for a nine-day trip.

He stares at me for a minute and then pastes a smile on his face. "Forget it. Just make sure you don't stack everything so I can't see out the back window. Oh, and make sure we can easily get to the shit we need for hotel stops each night. I don't wanna have to go digging for anything."

With that, he stalks toward the kitchen. I watch as he grabs a beer out of the fridge and twists the top off. As he drinks half of the bottle down in one gulp, anger stirs in my gut.

"Sure, drink so I have to drive," I mumble under my breath.

He knows it's hard for me to see at night, but doesn't he give a crap? Nope.

It takes another hour and a half for me to get my books, preorders, swag, and luggage loaded into the car. And just because he pissed me off, I shove the duffel with Rod's stuff on the passenger seat floor. Let's see how comfy he gets then.

As I head to my office to get some writing done before we leave, my cell phone vibrates in my pocket. I pull it out and grin when I see it's Darcie.

"Hey, lady."

"I had a quick break, so I figured I'd call and go over your signing checklist with you," she says.

"I'm good," I assure her. "Everything is in the car and ready to go."

"You're sure?"

"Of course I'm sure, Dar."

"Then you won't mind if I go over the checklist."

"It's your break to waste I guess."

"Exactly," she says with a laugh. "Laptop?"

"Check."

"At least fifteen copies of each book?"

"Check."

"Giveaway basket?"

"Check."

"The case with all your swag?"

"Check."

"Did you remember to put the new bookmarks you got yesterday in there?"

"Check." I chuckle. "I didn't forget an—"

"The backup charger for your cell phone?"

I search my memory for an image of me putting the extra charger in my suitcase, but it's not there. Shit.

"I knew it," Darcie says. "I knew you'd forget something."

"Fine, I forgot." I yank open my desk drawer and pull out the charger. "Well, go on. Go through the rest."

It takes another ten minutes to get through the list, and Darcie covers everything from books to sunscreen. There were five more things I forgot.

"Hey, I gotta run, Nova. But be safe and let me know when you get to Texas."

"You know we won't get there until Friday, right? That's three days from now."

"Okay, then text me every night when you stop," she says. "Just make sure I know you're safe," she tacks on.

"You know I will."

My stomach growls as I disconnect the call, so I grab a bag of chips from my desk. I rip them open and shove three in my mouth as I open up my latest work in progress.

He rests his hands on my hips and pulls me backward until my ass rubs against his cock. I'm still wet from my shower, but Donovan doesn't seem to care. I stare at our reflection in the bathroom mirror, and his tanned skin looks darker than it really is next to my pale flesh, but it works. We work.

"What are you waiting for?" I purr. "Fuck my ass, big boy."

I groan as I read the last line I wrote before stopping last night.

Big boy? Really, Nova?

Leaning back in my chair, I think about the books I read and how the sex scenes are written. There are times they fall short for me, and as an author, I get it. I mean, how many ways can you describe the act of sex? But then there are others that have me reaching for Cyrus, my trusty vibrating boyfriend, because they're not only creative, but they make me want to try wicked things.

An idea starts to form so I polish off the last of my chips and toss the empty bag in the trash can under my desk. Then I delete that last line and begin typing.

"What are you waiting for?" I purr as I wiggle against him.

Donovan's nostrils flare, and he slides a hand over my hip and up my back. With his palm pressing my spine, he pushes me down until my chest is flat against the counter. The cool granite is a stark contrast to the heat flowing through my veins.

"Have you been a good girl, Cori?" he growls. "Because good girls get their ass fucked. Bad girls get spanked."

"I-I don't know." I shiver, but it has nothing to do with temperature.

"Hmmm." Donovan holds me down as he rubs a circle over my ass cheek. "Wrong answer."

I swear my pussy weeps when he spanks me, and I whimper.

"You like that, Cori?"

I nod.

Donovan spanks me again. "Use your words, baby," he commands.

"Y-yes, I liked that."

I pause to read back through the words I've typed, and my own pussy pulses with need. But it's not Rod I want feeding my desire. Nope, I'm an idiot and want a fictional man who only exists in my own fucking head.

The struggle is real.

Staring at the document on my computer screen, I can't help but wonder if men like Donovan Kissinger actually exist in the real world.

Highly unlikely.

An image of the man in the diner last week pops into my mind, and I squirm in my chair. My clit throbs as I remember the way his dark eyes focused on me the entire time I was eating, at the way his gaze turned savage anytime Rod did something questionable. Could the man tell when I was annoyed? Was he able to see through my fake smiles?

I push the thoughts of him out of my brain and force myself to focus on my novel. No good can come from lusting over a man who lives his life on the edge. The second I spotted him, with his neck tattoo and cut, I knew he was a biker. And bikers don't have trysts with level-headed authors who write about fictional bikers. That shit doesn't happen.

Does it?

With a groan, I start typing, throwing every ounce of my very vivid fantasies into the fictitious world that pays my bills. Forty-two hundred words later, I have two more chapters completed and an ache in my chest that I worry will never go away because it's been a constant since I learned fairy tales aren't real.

And neither are biker romances.

I go through the motions of shutting down my computer and turning everything off in my office. After closing and locking the door, I make my way to the living room. Rod is in the same spot he was in earlier, only now he's sleeping.

For a split-second, I consider leaving without him, but

then dismiss the idea. The fact of the matter is, I need his help. But even if I didn't, nothing would change. Despite how frustrated I get with him, Rod isn't a terrible person, and I know he loves me in his own way. He's just lazy with a side of temper sometimes.

Besides, it's not like I want forever with him. Or with anyone for that matter. Relationships aren't perfect, and if I strive for that, I'll only end up more disappointed.

"Rod," I call as I shake him awake. "We gotta hit the road."

It takes a minute for him to come around, but when he does, he smiles. And that smile is exactly what sucked me in when we first met. So I focus on that, on the good times.

"Wow, sorry, Nov." He rubs his eyes. "Didn't mean to fall asleep."

"I know. It's okay." Grabbing his hand, I tug him to his feet. "But we've gotta get going."

"Okay."

Ten minutes later, we're walking out the front door. I decide to drive the first leg of the trip, so Rod climbs into the passenger seat.

"Seriously?" he says when he kicks his duffel bag. "You couldn't fit this in the back with the rest?"

I shrug. "I wanted to make sure you could see out the back window like you said."

Rod's good mood takes a nose-dive. "Always the smart ass." He lifts his bag onto his lap and yanks open the zipper. After digging around for a minute, he huffs out a breath. "We gotta run by my apartment real quick."

And there goes my good mood.

"Seriously Rod? We don't have time for detours. I have everything planned out because I have to be at the resort by a spe—"

"I'll be quick," he snaps.

I back out of the driveway and head in the opposite direction from the interstate. It takes twenty minutes to get to Rod's apartment building, and after I park, he rushes inside and up to his fifth-floor unit.

As I wait, I scroll through social media and respond to a few messages from readers and post about hitting the road for the Motorcycle, Mobsters, and Mayhem signing. I'm so focused on my frustration with Rod and my cell phone that I fail to notice the group of motorcycles parked in the lot or the dark eyes that are watching me and my boyfriend's every move.

Chapter Four
LEAD

"There he is."

I stare at our target as he runs across the parking lot. We've been sitting here for an hour, and I was about to give up and read my brothers the riot act for bringing me on a fool's errand.

"What the fuck?"

I turn to look at Arrow, who's not watching Rod. Following his gaze, I stiffen when I see what, or who, he's focused on.

"What is she doing here?" I ask because Nova Stone—I may or may not have glanced at her social media profile as soon as I returned to the clubhouse after seeing her at the diner—is sitting in her car, with the light of her cell phone illuminating her features.

Arrow pulls out his cell and taps on the screen a few times before shaking his head. "She just posted that she's on her way to Texas for some book signing thingy."

"That's not wh—" I press my lips into a thin line before I say too much. No need for them to know I turned into a cyber stalker.

"Yeah, her assistant is going with her," Brew adds.

"Does it look like her assistant is with her?" I bark.

"Prez, we did the leg work," Kicker, our Sergeant at Arms insists. "The girlfriend leaving for Texas is why we chose tonight to deal with Rod. He shoulda been home alone."

"Well, he hasn't been fucking home at all until now," I snap. "And he's definitely not alone."

"It's your call, Prez," Mercenary says. "We can back out and hit him another time."

Movement catches my attention out of the corner of my eye. I swivel my head and watch Rod stride back toward the car with a death grip on the strap of a backpack. He climbs into the passenger side of Nova's vehicle and a few minutes later, they pull out onto the road.

"Prez?" Arrow prompts.

"We follow them."

I fire up my Harley, and the others do the same.

"Kicker and Toot, head back to the clubhouse and grab the SUVs and our go bags. Also, reach out to Fender with the Soulless Kings and see if he can have brothers from any of their chapters meet us en route to pick up our bikes and keep them stored at their clubhouse until we return."

"You're gonna trust the SKs with our fucking Harleys?" Brick snaps.

"We trust them with Charlie and Sylvia," I remind him. "Or are you forgetting the truce that was called when Charlie shacked up with Fender?"

"No, Prez, I didn't forget."

"Good. Now fucking go so we can catch up to Rod," I order.

Kicker and Toot both nod before tearing out of the lot and heading toward the clubhouse. I pull out my cell and share my location so they can catch up to us later. After shoving the phone back into my cut, I lift my hand in the air and swing it in a circle.

"Let's ride, brothers!"

Brew and I take the lead, with Arrow and Mercenary behind us and Brick behind them. We stay back enough that we aren't immediately recognized as tailing the couple, but not so far that we lose them.

Two hours later, Nova takes an exit and pulls into a McDonald's parking lot. We head to the gas station across the street.

"Yo, Prez," Arrow calls as he gets off his bike to stretch his legs. "Just got a text from Kicker. He said Fender's on board. He'll have a few of his brothers from their Twin Falls, Idaho chapter meet up with us somewhere. We just have to text their Prez when we're near there."

"Great. Are he and Toot back on the road?"

"'Bout an hour and a half behind us. They've got your location, so they'll catch up."

With my eyes on Nova's car across the street, I absently nod. "No clue when we'll be stopping again boys so I suggest you take care of business if you have to."

I have to take a leak, but I can't bring myself to let the car or the woman driving it out of my sight. Rather than head inside with the others, I move to the side of the gas station to find relief. As I pull up my zipper, Nova and Rod come out of the fast-food restaurant.

Moving to the entrance, I pound on the door to get my brothers' attention, and then get back on my Harley. In a matter of minutes, we're once again following the pretty author and her sack-of-shit boyfriend.

Kicker and Toot catch up with us, and six and a half hours later, we reach the outskirts of Twin Falls. Fortunately, there are several chain hotels at the exit Nova chooses, and we're able to stay at one down the road that offers us a view of her car.

Several Soulless Kings arrive twenty minutes later to pick up our bikes, and I only issue four threats of death if any harm comes to our machines. Despite assuring Brick that we can trust our Harleys with another club, I'm not completely confident that that's the case. I don't think they'd do anything intentionally, but accidents happen.

"You gonna get some sleep, Prez?"

I straighten from my position against the wall and push past Arrow. While the others checked into their rooms, I admitted to myself that sleep would be futile. There's no way I'd be able to relax knowing that Nova is likely lying next to a dead man walking.

"I'm good," I snap, shoving a hand through my hair.

Arrow huffs out a humorless laugh. "Bullshit." I glare at him, and he shrugs one shoulder. "You're not good, Lead. You're a walking, snarling ball of not fucking good."

"What the fuck is that supposed to mean?"

"Ever since you laid eyes on that bitch," Arrow says with a nod toward the hotel Nova is staying in. "You've been acting like a man who wants to burn down the world."

"What makes you think it's because of her?" I counter. "Her boyfriend owes my club money. That doesn't exactly promote happiness."

"Yet this is the first time you've involved yourself with someone so insignificant on our list." He holds a hand up when I open my mouth to speak. "I'm not complaining. You're the Prez and have every right to be as involved as you want, I just can't help but wonder why. And the only thing that makes sense is the girl."

"Leave it alone," I bark.

"You need to get her outta your head, man. By all accounts, she's a nice girl. You'd break her, Lead. You'd break her like a damn cowboy breaks a wild mustang, leaving her a shell of whoever the hell she is now."

Nice girl? How the hell would he know? Because her books paint a very different picture.

But I can't say that. I can't admit that, along with stalking her social media, I bought one of her books and started reading it on my phone. There is nothing *nice* about them.

"Leave. It. Alone," I repeat.

"Fine." He shoves his hands in his pockets. "I'm gonna try and catch some shut eye. Brew will be down to relieve you in a few hours."

I absently nod, my mind spiraling into the worlds created by Nova Stone. Arrow finally leaves me alone, and I take up my place against the wall.

You'd break her, Lead.

Would I? Maybe. Probably. Almost certainly.

The dedication in the book I've been reading flashes in my brain like a giant neon sign.

For anyone who learned the hard way that fairy tales don't exist. Real men may let you down, but a book boyfriend never will.

You'd break her, Lead.

But would I? She already doesn't believe in all that frilly, lovey-dovey shit. And if the men in her book are anything to go by, maybe I'm exactly what she believes in.

I dig out my cell and open the book to the last page I read. If I'm going to stay awake, I might as well be entertained.

Chapter Five
NOVA

"Gimme a damn minute!"

I stomp my foot in agitation before striding across the room and throwing myself on the bed. Rod has been in the bathroom for thirty minutes already, and I still need to shower. I've already consumed all of the coffee in the room, knowing it's going to be another long night of driving, so not only do I have to shower, but I also have to fucking pee.

This whole driving at night thing is throwing off my rhythm. But hopefully, after this next stretch, it'll right itself again. We've got almost fourteen hours to go until we stop in Raton, New Mexico, but we'll be staying there long enough that it'll be morning when we hit the road again.

"Dear God, how long does it ta—"

"It's all yours," Rod says after stepping out of the bathroom.

"About time," I mutter as I push off the bed.

When I move past Rod, he grabs my arm and pulls me toward him. "What did you say?"

He's narrowing his eyes at me, and there's a gleam in them

that I don't recognize. I try to yank free, but he tightens his grip.

What the hell?

"Let me go," I demand.

Rod stares, but it's as if he's looking through me instead of at me. I wiggle my arm, and he seems to snap out of it. He quickly releases me and shakes his head.

"Quit with the attitude, Nova," he bites out. "I'm not in the mood."

I don't know what to say to that, so I step away from him and go into the bathroom, closing the door behind me. Without hesitation, I twist the lock. I've never felt the need to lock him out of a room before, but that whole thirty-second interaction was... weird.

Wanting to get on the road as soon as possible, I take a quick shower. I dress in a pair of black leggings, a red tank top, and a pair of red flip-flops. The further south we get, the warmer it gets, and I hate being hot in the car. I don't bother drying my hair, choosing instead to pull it up into a messy bun.

Twenty minutes later, I'm at the front desk checking out, and Rod is sitting in the car outside the entrance. The engine is running and from the looks of it, he's already asleep in the passenger seat.

I debate on waking him up to make him drive but decide against it. The more he sleeps, the less I have to worry about my *attitude*.

As I navigate my way toward the interstate, anxiety creeps in. Motorcycles, Mobsters, and Mayhem is the biggest event I've been invited to sign at, and without Darcie, I'm not sure how I'm going to manage. Not only does she anticipate my every need, but she also brings me out of my shell in a way others can't.

Fortunately, my table is next to Jessa Aarons. We don't

know each other very well, but that doesn't seem to matter. Being an author can be a very lonely, isolating career so when you meet others in the industry, you foster those relationships and connections the best you can online.

Kristine Allen is assigned to the other table next to me. I've met her once, and she's sweet as can be. Being so close to her will pose a bit of a problem though... I'll be so busy fangirling over her that I worry I'll miss readers fangirling over me.

Not a bad problem to have, Novalyn.

Rod begins to stir awake after an hour, and my stomach twists into knots. I chalk it up to the way he manhandled me at the hotel.

"Where are we?" he asks as he turns to look out all the windows. "Are we almost there?"

I snort. "Not even close."

"Then where are we?"

I lift my phone to show him the GPS. "See that little blue arrow?"

"Yeah."

"That's where we are."

Rod leans forward and grabs the bag he insisted he keep up front with him. He rifles through it, becoming more agitated as the seconds pass, but he must find what he's looking for because he releases an audible breath and rests his head against his seat.

"I need you to stop as soon as you can."

I glance at him out of the corner of my eye as my grip tightens on the steering wheel.

"We've only been on the road an hour, Rod," I tell him. "Can't it wait?"

"I've gotta piss," he snaps.

"Okay. Calm down. I'll stop."

It's another ten miles before we come up on an exit, and

before I can even put the car in park at the twenty-four-hour gas station, Rod is throwing open his door and running inside. Taking advantage of the stop, I lift my cell and, ignoring the fact that it's the middle of the night, send a text to Darcie.

> Me: Wish you were here. Gonna be a long trip with R.

I don't expect her to reply, so I switch to social media and scroll through the latest posts in the event group. I'm about to comment on a reader's post about what everyone is wearing for the meet and greet when my phone pings with a text notification.

> Darcie: Don't let him steal your fun.

> Me: I'm trying. But he's being a dick.

> Darcie: He's always a dick.

I heave a sigh. It does me no good to argue with her. She doesn't like Rod, and nothing I do or say will change that.

> Me: Go back to bed. I'll call you later.

> Darcie: Be safe.

> Me: Always.

I bring up the GPS on my cell and tuck the device under my thigh. Rod has been inside for much longer than the time it takes to pee and my annoyance doubles. He's wasting precious time.

He returns to the vehicle five minutes later, and he seems more relaxed.

"Let's go, babe."

With a roll of my eyes, I shift into gear.

Darcie's right... Rod is a dick.

"Damn."

Rod whistles as he stares out the windshield. I follow his gaze and resist the urge to smack him when I see the barely legal girls strutting across the parking lot in little more than scraps of cloth that are supposed to pass as bathing suits.

It took four hours longer than anticipated, but we've arrived at the resort where Motorcycles, Mobsters, and Mayhem is being held. I lost track of the number of times Rod demanded I stop for one reason or another.

"I'm gonna go check in." I grab my purse and phone before opening the door. "Make yourself useful and find one of those hotel cart thingies so we can get everything to the room in one trip."

Six more days, Nova. Just six more days.

Rather than wait for some smart-ass comment from him or to see if he actually does anything, I make my way inside the resort lobby. The place is packed. It's practically wall-to-wall full of authors, readers, and... bikers.

For the first time since we left Oregon a giant grin splits my face. Fairy tales might not exist, but fantasies sure as hell do.

Pushing through the mass of leather and denim, I can't help but feel giddy at the unlimited supply of inspiration I'm now surrounded by. It doesn't get much better than this.

As I stand in line, I soak in the excitement buzzing through the air. I watch as other authors and their assistants, spouses, kids, or whoever they brought with them, lug in boxes and boxes of books, swag, and luggage. After I get through the motions of checking in and getting the room keys, I return to the vehicle.

Rod is standing at the rear with the trunk open, but nothing is unloaded and there is no hotel cart.

"What took you so long?" he barks when I get close.

I slowly look around us before leveling my stare on Rod. "Do you not see all the people here? It's busy, Rod."

"I see all the bikers and cover models," he gripes. "Sure you weren't chatting it up with any of them?"

I throw my hands up. "Like you were wanting to *chat up* the jailbait you were ogling when we parked?" With a shake of my head, I reach past him and grab a suitcase. "This is ridiculous. Can we just get to our room before you start complaining? I'd prefer not to make a scene."

"Where's our room?" he asks as he starts to take boxes out of the car and set them on the ground.

I tell him the room number and give him the same directions I was given. He grabs one of the keys from my hand and a suitcase before storming away, presumably to the room.

"Gee, thanks," I mutter to myself. "I can get the rest."

I finish unloading everything and then lock the car. Glancing around, I scan my surroundings for a cart but see none. Great, just fucking great.

Stacking the boxes, I try to figure out how I'm gonna get this all inside by myself because clearly, I can't count on Rod. I've got my wagon, but it won't hold everything.

"Need help?"

I whirl around toward the deep voice and almost swallow my tongue. Standing no more than three feet away is a real living, breathing version of one of my characters.

"Do you?" the man asks.

"D-do I what?" I stammer.

Jesus, I'm a mess.

"Need help getting all that to your room," he clarifies with a smirk.

"Oh, uh..." I shake my head. "Yeah, that'd be great. Thanks."

"Don't mention it," he says as he lifts a box.

His muscles bulge beneath his t-shirt, and I have to force myself to look away. I unfold the wagon so we can put some boxes in there, and the biker patiently waits.

"I hope that wasn't your boyfriend who left you to deal with this all on your own."

"Yep, afraid so."

"Dude needs a lesson in chivalry."

"He's not always like that," I insist. "It's been a long few days to get here. We're both ju—"

"He doesn't deserve your excuses, Darlin'."

My shoulders stiffen. I might be angry at Rod, and I might not always like how he acts, but he *is* my boyfriend. I don't appreciate people I care about being put down, especially by someone who doesn't even know them.

"Look, I appreciate your help," I begin. "But I really don't need the judgment."

He sets the box he was holding in the wagon and lifts another with a chuckle. "Okay."

The two of us work in silence to fill the wagon. He creatively stacks the boxes so most of them fit, and what doesn't, he carries as we move to the entrance.

When the doors slide open and we step inside, I see Rod walking across the lobby.

"What the hell, Nova?" he barks as his eyes dart from me to the biker then back to me. "You just couldn't wait, could you?"

"Rod, he—"

"Might want to watch how you talk to her," the biker

snaps. "Not sure you're surrounded by people who will be okay with your disrespect."

"And who the fuck are you?" Rod snaps.

"Nobody to concern yourself with." The man looks at me. "You got it from here?"

"Yeah," I assure him. "Thanks for the help."

"No problem, Darlin'."

With that, he walks away. I have to make a conscious effort not to stare at his ass, but I manage... barely.

"And that's why I didn't want you coming to this thing," Rod complains.

"Don't," I snap, at my wit's end. "Don't start."

He glares at me but doesn't say anything more. We get all of our stuff to the room, and he locks himself in the bathroom. I have no idea how long he's in there because as soon as I kick my flip-flops off, I lay on the bed and fall asleep.

Chapter Six

LEAD

"Holy shit."

I laugh at Toot, who's turning in slow circles and grinning like a fool at all the people. More specifically, at all the women. There are so many fucking women. But that's not at all surprising. The sheer number of Harleys and bikers is though.

"I'm so getting laid," Arrow says with what can only be described as a twinkle in his fucking eyes.

"Not it," Kicker says with a chuckle.

"Aw, c'mon," Arrow complains. "You love rooming with me."

"Not when you're face deep in pussy. And let's face it, you're gonna do everything you can to make sure that's exactly where you are." Kicker shakes his head. "So nope, not it. I am not sharing a room with you."

"Arrow and Mercenary are with me," I say absently. "The rest of you will share another room."

Toot throws back his head and laughs. "Guess you're not gettin' any, VP."

"Dammit, Prez," Arrow whines. "Just because you're not—"

"Do not finish that sentence," I bark as I smack Arrow upside the head. "We're here on club business. This isn't a goddamn pleasure trip."

"Speaking of business..." Brew nods toward the entrance. "Rod just went inside and left Nova with all that shit."

I squint against the sun and stare at the woman in question. She looks pissed as hell, and I push off the SUV with one thought in mind: go help her.

"Ooo, what do we have here?" Brick says and crosses his arms over his chest.

A man is now standing with Nova, and she appears flustered. "Looks like someone came to her rescue," I observe.

"Shoulda been you," Arrow says and when I glare at him, he shrugs.

"Let's go get us some rooms," I say and move to the back of the SUV to grab my bag.

"Shit, I forgot to tell you," Kicker says as he lifts his duffel. "I had Moose get us reservations. He should have emailed you the confirmation, Prez."

I pull my cell out of my cut and navigate to my email app. Sure enough, there's an email from Moose with the subject line 'Expensive fucking accommodations'.

Glancing back toward Nova's car, I see that she and the other man are gone. Disappointment settles in my gut, but I refuse to let it get to me. Besides, at least she didn't disappear with Rod.

But she will.

We head inside and stand in line to check in. The lobby is jam-packed, and the hairs on the back of my neck stand on end as the heads of females start to turn toward us.

"They're staring, Prez," Toot says.

"Chicks are fucking drooling," Brew agrees with a chuckle.

"Yeah, but... some of 'em are old enough to be my grandma." Kicker shudders.

Mercenary groans. "Dude, that's not always a bad thing. Grannies can get freaky as fuck."

I tune them out as they continue to debate the pros and cons of age and experience. There's only one woman I give a damn about when it comes to those things and that's...

Fuck my life.

How the hell did this girl dig her claws so fucking deep? I've never even spoken to her. All it took was one look and lightning struck. It doesn't make sense, and it's scary as hell, but there was an instant and almost desperate need to make her mine.

Which is how I find myself in goddamn Texas at a book signing when I should be back in Oregon. It's why I dragged my brothers on a run that could have waited until Rod returned home. And it's the reason I've got a fucking romance novel downloaded on my phone that I'm itching to finish reading.

"All set, Prez." Mercenary slaps me on the back, snapping me out of my thoughts.

We make our way through the crowd and my eyes are constantly scanning, constantly roving. I try to convince myself I'm only on alert like I always am, but I fail miserably. When we reach our rooms, which are across the hall from each other, we separate to settle in.

"What's the plan for tonight?" Mercenary asks after tossing his gear on the couch.

"Not much," I respond as I walk through the living area to the bedroom. "Sleep for a bit and then go from there."

Arrow starts to enter the bedroom but stops in his tracks when I narrow my eyes at him.

"You're taking the room all for yourself, aren't you?" he asks.

"What gave you that impression?" I counter with a smirk.

Arrow spins around and goes straight to the couch. He lifts Mercenary's bag and tosses it to the floor. "I outrank you, bro."

Mercenary chuckles and shakes his head. "I've slept in the desert with bombs and gunfire going off around me. You really think I give a shit about sleeping on a damn floor?"

"I'm gonna sleep for a few hours," I tell them both with my hand on the door. "Anything comes up, handle it."

After slamming the door, I stride to the bed. As I stretch across the mattress, I pull my cell out to call Moose. He answers on the second ring.

"Yo, Prez. Get checked in okay?"

"Yeah," I tell him. "Thanks for making the reservation."

"No problem. How's Texas?"

"Hot as hell."

"The weather or the chicks?"

I chuckle. "Both. Anything going on there?"

"Nah. The highlight of the last three days was going to the diner."

"How is that a highlight?"

"Because watching Whiz try to convince Kit that he's bigger than Arrow without actually whipping his dick out is fucking hilarious."

"I bet Kit loved that."

"She got a kick out of it. Bitch is wicked." He sighs dramatically. "If we ever run out of ways to put the prospects in their place, Kit's got our backs."

"Yeah, sounds like Kit. Anything else I should know?"

"Nope. We've got things covered here."

"Call if you need anything. But please, try not to need anything."

"You got it, Prez."

We disconnect the call, and I open the stupid app I had to download to read Nova's book. Scooting up the mattress so I can prop myself up against the pillows, I pick up where I left off.

Within minutes, I'm lost in a fictional world that is surprisingly not that dissimilar from the real world.

Chapter Seven

NOVA

"Well, that sucked."

Rod and I are on our way back to the resort after having dinner with a few other authors and their husbands and assistants. And he's right, it sucked. But only because he was a complete prick, and it was obvious he was making the others uncomfortable.

"I swear those guys are whipped," he continues. "There's no way they're that into all this book bullshit."

I tighten my grip on the steering wheel and press my lips together to keep from lashing out. It took every ounce of self-control not to toss my beer in his face at the restaurant, but I'm wishing I would've. Maybe then I wouldn't be so tempted to push him out of the car.

"I just don't get it. I mean, what kinda man gets excited about character names, cover designs, and—"

"A man who gives a damn about the woman he loves," I snap as I jerk the wheel to the right and slam on the brakes on the side of the road.

"What the hell are you doing?"

I put the car in park and twist in my seat to glare at Rod.

"What is going on with you lately?" I spit out. "I know you don't get what I do for a living, but you've never been this deliberately cruel." When he simply stares at me, I continue. "We've been together for a while, Rod, and I've never expected poetry and grand gestures, but I also won't put up with you being downright mean. I've about had enough."

"Nothing is going on with me."

Out of all I said, that's what he chooses to focus on?

I want to argue with him, but what's the point? He clearly doesn't understand why I'm angry, and I'm starting to wonder if he even cares.

There's a reason you don't believe in fairy tales.

Besides, even if there was a point, there's no time. The meet and greet starts in twenty minutes and we're still fifteen miles away.

Facing forward, I shift the car into drive and pull back onto the road. Not even two minutes pass before my phone starts ringing. Since I'm driving, I ignore it, but Rod doesn't. He reaches for my cell and because I'm navigating through Friday evening traffic, I can't stop him.

"Hello?" He pauses for a second before sighing. "Oh, hey Dee... Yeah, she's right here." He holds the device out to me. "It's your mom."

I shake my head but rather than take the hint, Rod taps the screen and holds the phone between us. "You're on speaker, Dee."

I'm gonna kill him. I'm gonna wrap my fingers around his throat and squeeze until the life drains from—

"Novalyn, are you almost here?" Mom asks.

After a few deep breaths, I ask, "Where?"

Mom laughs, and the sound grates on my already frayed nerves. "That's not funny. The rehearsal dinner starts in ten minutes, and I was expecting you to be here by now."

"You're getting married?" Rod asks.

Fingers, throat, life draining...

"Well of course I am, Rodney," she trills. "Which is why I'm confused as to why my daughter isn't here already."

"Mom, I told you I wasn't going to be there," I remind her. "I'm in Texas for work."

She gasps, and I roll my eyes. "I didn't think you were serious about that."

"About my work?" I ask.

"About you choosing it over me."

"Look, I can't do this right now, Mom. I told you I couldn't be there. I'm not sure why my presence matters anyway. It's not like the marriage will stick."

Immediately I want to call the words back. The fact that she flits from man to man doesn't give me license to disrespect her. I don't hate the woman. I just wish she wasn't so selfish.

"I'm sorry, Mom," I say when she doesn't utter a word. "That was uncalled for."

There's a brief pause and then she sniffles, thrusting the knife of guilt into my chest. "I need to go. Goodbye, Novalyn."

The line goes silent, and my shoulders slump as Rod slides the cell under my thigh.

"Why didn't you tell me she was getting married?" he asks, sounding genuinely curious.

I heave a sigh. "I did, Rod."

Reaching for the knob, I turn the radio on and crank up the volume. I half expect Rod to turn it down and argue with me, but he doesn't, and I'm grateful. The last thing I need right now is to worry about my mom and Rod. There will be time enough for both after the event.

A few minutes later we arrive at the resort. After parking, I rush toward the entrance, and Rod follows. Before we make it to the elevator, he slips his arm around my waist and guides me to the edge of the lobby.

"I'm sorry, Nova," he says as he tugs me into his side. "I have a lot on my mind and shouldn't take it out on you."

Whiplash. He's gonna give me whiplash with the shifts in attitude.

"I think I'll stay in the room while you go to your thing," he says when I remain quiet. "I'm not up for more socializing, and you don't need me hovering."

Relief floods my system, and I nod. "Works for me."

He leans down and kisses me. The contact is short and lacks even the slightest hint of the spark I once felt with him.

"I'll see ya later," he says, and he removes his arm.

"Okay." He starts to walk away, but I halt him with my words "Oh, don't forget we set up tonight. I'll need your help with that."

Rod's shoulders tense, but he nods without looking at me. Then he continues toward the elevator. Once the doors close behind him, it's as if a giant weight has been lifted. I'm not thrilled to be going to the meet and greet alone, but I'm more than a little happy about going without him.

The meet and greet is overwhelming at first, but I quickly settle into the rhythm of introductions and comfortable conversations. It's not hard to forget my anxiety when the common thread among every person in the room is our love of all things books.

Around nine, Sapphire Knight, one of the signing authors and the host of the event, announces that we can get into the ballroom to set up for tomorrow. While it's not required to set up tonight, I much prefer it so I'm not all sweaty and nasty as readers are hugging me and asking for pictures.

I make my way to the elevator, not paying attention to my surroundings. When the doors slide open and I step inside, I realize I'm not alone. I glance at the panel of buttons and see that the man presses the same floor I need, so I step back and lean against the side as we ascend. And the entire time I covertly check him out.

He's standing so I can see his profile, and he looks familiar, but I can't place him. He's wearing a cut, but I don't recognize any of the patches on the front. I dismiss the idea that I know him, telling myself it's impossible. I've never been to Texas, and I don't know any bikers.

But there's one you can't forget, one who has plagued your dreams since you saw him at the diner.

We reach our floor, and the doors open. I push off the wall to follow him off but freeze when I see the back of his cut. I'd recognize that design, that club name anywhere. Because the man who's invaded my every sleeping thought wears the same one.

Black Savages MC.

What the hell are they doing here?

The man who stepped off the elevator glances over his shoulder and smiles. The sense of familiarity deepens, and now I know why. I must have seen him back home at some point. He's not my biker though.

Wait... does this mean my biker is here? Is he close?

My biker?

"You comin'?" the man asks.

I shake my head free of my thoughts.

"No?" He arches a brow and turns to face me completely.

"Uh, yeah," I push out. "Yeah, I'm coming."

His quizzical expression shifts, and he smirks as he lowers his gaze as if sizing me up. His perusal is slow, but it doesn't feel sexual. Sure, his eyes pause on my tits and between my legs, but it doesn't bother me. Not like it should.

"Dammit," he mutters, and then he grins. "I get it."

"Get what?"

"Nothing. I'm Arrow, by the way."

I shake his offered hand. "Nova. It's uh, nice to meet you."

"You too." We start down the hall. "Are you here for this book signing thing?" he asks.

"Yeah. I'm an author," I say proudly.

"Cool." He stops two doors before mine. "Well, this is me. Have a good night, Nova."

"You too."

He disappears into his room, and I go to mine. When I open the door, I brace myself for an argument from Rod about needing his help setting up. But I quickly realize I'm bracing for the wrong disappointment. Because my boyfriend is nowhere to be seen.

Son of a bitch.

Chapter Eight

LEAD

I tip the tumbler of whiskey to my lips and down the contents in one long gulp. When Arrow came back to the suite and told me he'd run into Nova, jealousy slithered around my body like a boa constrictor coiling around its prey. It was quickly followed by rage at him having been seen by her.

"Can I get you another?"

I hand the bartender the glass and nod. "Thanks."

Arrow explained that she didn't seem to know who he was, which calmed me a bit, but then he told me that Rod was at one of the resort bars flirting with some chick who was most definitely not his girlfriend.

"Here ya go." The bartender sets a fresh drink in front of me.

I sip on this one as I watch the scene unfolding across the bar. Rod is standing at a high-top table between the long legs of a woman who's sitting on a stool. He has his arms wrapped around her waist, and he's laughing at something she's saying.

Mercenary was here keeping an eye on the prick, but I excused him when I got to the bar. I wanted to go straight to

Nova and tell her what her boyfriend was doing, so taking over for Mercenary was the only way to ensure I didn't do that. Someone needs to keep eyes on Rod.

Okay, so not really. But it's what I keep telling myself so I don't rush to Nova's room like a fool.

Rod interacts with the woman for another hour or so, and when they start toward the exit, I toss a few bills down onto the bar to cover my tab and follow. She leads him up a set of stairs, stopping several times to make out against the wall.

I could easily take him out here and now, but then I'd have to deal with the bitch. Too messy. And there are too many damn people at this event to be certain no one else would stumble upon us as I take his life from him.

It takes twenty minutes, but they finally reach a room I can only assume is hers because it's definitely not the one he's sharing with Nova. They disappear inside, and I pull out my cell to text Kicker.

> Me: Suite 418... get here

I don't want to go to Nova like a child and tattle on her man, but I don't want to stand here for fuck knows how long while he gets his rocks off either. That's what I've got brothers for.

My phone vibrates, and I look at the notification.

> Kicker: On my way

Shoving my cell into my back pocket, I lean against the wall and wait. It doesn't take long for my Sergeant at Arms to arrive, and when he does, I return to the bar to drink away my frustration.

I'm two shots and three more glasses of whiskey deep when I sense someone behind me. I slide the glass in my hand away from me and prepare to grab the knife out of my boot should it become necessary.

"Any other time, and you'd have had that blade pressed against my carotid artery."

I whirl around and glare at Arrow. His arms are crossed over his chest, and he's looking at me like he's disappointed.

Join the motherfucking club.

"I knew it was you," I grumble and turn back to face the bar. I lift my hand to the bartender, and he nods to let me know he sees me. "Whaddya want, VP?"

"Nothing," he says and sits on the stool next to me. "Figured it was better to come here and drink than to raid the mini bar. Shorty would have a fucking fit if he saw those charges on the bill."

I snort. "He wouldn't have a fit. He'd rip your balls off."

"And you'd let him, wouldn't you?"

"Damn straight. You know I hate to have the club's money wasted."

"Yet, we're in Texas on a run involving a man who owes the club under ten grand." He arches a brow at me. "You don't think that's a waste of club resources?"

The bartender sets another tumbler in front of me, and I down it before he can even turn away. Holding the glass out again, I shake the ice to indicate I want another.

"Of course, it's a waste of goddamn resources," I snap when the bartender walks away. "Despite my recent actions, I'm not an idiot."

"Right. And I'm not a horny bastard who'd rather be under some chick riding my face than here talking to you." His tone is full of sarcasm which only darkens my already black mood.

"I'm not stopping you," I snap.

"Actually, you are, Prez. You specifically told us we aren't here for fun and fucking. We're on club business. I know I joke around a lot, but I don't take my position lightly. I can hit up Kit when we get home to relieve some... pressure. Right now, I'm more concerned with how the hell we get home."

"Same way we got here," I say sarcastically. "Cage it to Twin Falls and ride our Harleys the rest of the way."

"That's not what I meant."

"What do you want from me, Arrow?" I bark, causing several heads to swivel our way.

"I want you to stop acting like some lovesick jackass and start acting like the president of a one-percenter MC."

"I'm not lovesick," I counter.

And I'm not. Love doesn't have shit to do with how I'm acting or the decisions I'm making. Love is an illusion, a fictional concept that only appears in books and fairy tales.

"Fine," he says. "Poor choice of words. But you get my drift."

"It sounds like you don't trust my judgment."

"I trust you with my life, and you know it. But our business with Rod can't be done here, not with all these people around."

"So... what? We go back to Oregon and sit on our hands and wait? Is that what you're suggesting?"

"I'm suggesting we figure out a plan so we're not wasting our time," he barks.

"We watch and wait. That's the plan."

"It's a damn shitty plan, Prez." Arrow grabs the fresh drink the bartender brings me and downs it himself. Then he takes out his wallet and tosses two hundred bucks on the bar. "C'mon, Lead. You need to sleep this off. We can figure something out in the morning."

"You seem to be forgetting who the fuck you're talking to," I snap, pissed off at the way he's ordering me around like I don't outrank him.

He simply shakes his head. "Yeah, and so do you."

He's right, of course. I'm acting like a dipshit. I know it, he knows it. Hell, the entire club probably knows it. Arrow is just the only one with balls big enough to call me on it. It's why he's my second in command. He doesn't pull any punches, even with me. Every leader needs someone like him in their corner.

My mind wanders to Nova, and I wonder who she has in her corner. Her social media is full of posts with her friend and assistant, a woman named Darcie. And she has Rod. But Rod's a drug-addicted cheater with an expiration date, and Darcie isn't here.

That leaves me. I'm in her corner. Well, I want to be anyway.

"Can I ask you something?" Arrow looks at me expectantly as we wait for the elevator, and I nod. "What is it about her that has you so worked up? I mean, she's fucking hot, don't get me wrong. But you don't know anything about her. You've never even spoken to her as far as I know."

I search my brain for an answer that'll make sense to him but come up empty. There isn't any possible combination of words that I can string together in a way he'd understand. He's a player, a dirty bastard who cares about getting his rocks off and the club and not much else.

But I have to try. Because I need someone, anyone, to understand.

My memory flashes to the dedication about real men and book boyfriends. It flashes to scenes in her book.

"I know that she's got walls up so high because she was hurt by someone. I know that she doesn't believe in love, but she wants to. I know she has a freaky side that she hides from the world, and she doesn't trust easily." I shrug. "I know enough to want to learn more."

"And you got all that from seeing her in the diner, from

tailing her to Texas and watching her like a creepy fucking hawk?"

"No, I—"

I press my lips together when the elevator opens and the object of my hatred steps on. Rod's sporting a grin, and he's got lipstick on his neck. I see red.

"Looks like someone got lucky," I comment, seething with a rage I've never experienced before.

The man puffs out his chest and chuckles. "You could say that."

Arrow and I exchange a look, and my VP's eyes bore into mine, silently pleading with me to not be stupid. I fail to see how choking the life out of Rod is stupid, but I won't do it. Not when I know there are cameras that would catch the act.

"You look familiar," I say, keeping my tone even.

Rod glances over his shoulder and studies me for a moment before shaking his head. "You don't."

Well, I guess we can count ourselves lucky for that. It's not surprising, considering there are always at least two or three middlemen between the club and the junkies who snort or shoot up our product. But I have to admit that a very small part of me wishes he did know who we were. Because then he'd know why we're here, he'd know his every move was being clocked and calculated in some random formula to determine how close to the end he really is.

Death has marked him, and I'm the reaper who's going to savagely collect.

Chapter Nine

NOVA

"Hey, do you need some help?"

I flash Jessa a grateful smile and try not to let the tears fall. Rod wasn't around to help me set up last night, and he's still not here for the start of the signing like he promised when I left the room a little while ago.

"I think I'm good, but thanks."

"Isn't Rod coming today?" Kristine asks as she steps up next to me. "I thought he was here as your assistant."

I huff out a humorless laugh. "He is. He, uh, drank a little too much last night. He should be here soon though."

Why the hell am I making excuses for him?

Because that's what you do for someone you care about.

Although, he's making it very hard to care about him lately.

"Nova, the guy's a dick," Rebecca, Jessa's assistant, says unashamedly. When the others give her a stern look, she shrugs. "I'm sorry, but he is. He had not one supportive thing to say to you at dinner last night. He wasn't at the meet and greet, and he didn't help you set up. You've gotta ditch him, girl."

"He's not always that bad," I insist, but even I can hear the lie in my words.

Okay, it's not an outright lie. Rod isn't always like he was last night. Or at least, he didn't used to be. I've never wanted a future with him because let's face it, what's the point? So I don't know why I'm resisting the idea of dumping him. Maybe it's the whole 'devil you know' concept, or maybe I'm a glutton for punishment. Either way, this isn't the time or place to try and sort through it.

"Listen up everyone!"

We all turn to face the middle of the room where Sapphire is standing on a chair.

"We're about to open the doors for VIP ticket holders. After an hour, we'll let general admission ticket holders in. Things are about to get crazy." She grins "I know some of you are nervous, but just remember to have fun. And if you need anything, don't hesitate to try and track me down or ask your fellow authors. We're all in this together."

Cheers and clapping fill the room, and my own excitement builds. Fuck Rod. Just because he's hell-bent on making this as difficult as possible for me doesn't mean I have to let him drag me down. Being here is an accomplishment I'm proud of, and he can't take that away from me, no matter how giant of an asshole he is.

Each author moves to their own table, and I settle behind mine. Even with the excitement I'm experiencing, I'm nervous.

You've got this, Novalyn. You write amazing books, and readers agree. Just be yourself.

The first hour goes by in a blur, but what a blur it is. I'm selling books at a rate I didn't realize was possible for me, and the readers are incredible. Another thirty minutes pass before Rod shows his face.

He flops down in the chair next to mine, the one I haven't occupied since the doors opened, and sighs as if he's inconvenienced by being here.

"Where the hell have you been?" I whisper harshly after several readers move on to Kristine's table.

"Chill, Nova," Rod says casually. "I was tired, so I slept in. It's not a big deal."

"Not a big—"

"Holy shit, it's you."

I paste a smile on my face and lift my head to look at the grinning woman in front of my table. She appears to be trying very hard not to bounce out of her shoes, and I love it.

"I mean, you're her," she says and lifts a paperback copy of my most recent release, *Uncaged*. She points to my picture on the back cover. "You're Nova Stone. I can't believe it."

My smile widens. "I am Nova Stone." I reach out to shake her hand. She hesitates for a moment, and then settles her hand in mine. "And you are?"

"Mandy," she says giddily. "Wow. I... Can I get a picture of you?"

Rod snorts from beside me, but I ignore him... for now.

"Of course. But why don't we get one together?" I suggest.

"Oh, right, yeah," she says. "That's what I meant." She taps her cell phone screen and thrusts the device at Rod. "Here, can you take it?"

"Just do it like a selfie," he says flippantly.

I glare at him, but he doesn't notice because he's too busy on his own cell phone. I'm so shocked by his blatant rudeness to a fan that I can't form any words. Hell, I can't make myself move.

"Um..."

"Here, let me take that for ya." I whip my head up and see Nikki Landis cross the narrow path between the rows and grab the reader's phone. "Nova, come stand in front of your banner with her," she instructs.

Nikki snaps the photo and returns the phone to Mandy.

"Thank you," Mandy and I say simultaneously.

"No problem." Nikki steps close to my table and leans toward Rod. "Get your goddamn head out of your ass and help your girlfriend." She glances over her shoulder as if scanning the room. "Before someone else does it for you."

With that, she returns to her table and interacts with her own fans as if the last two minutes didn't even happen. As for Mandy, I sign *Uncaged* for her, as well as the other five books she purchases before she moves on.

"That was rude," Rod snaps when she's gone.

"Yeah, it was," I say, not bothering to correct him when I know he's thinking I'm referring to Nikki.

Two hours pass without incident, but also without Rod helping me whatsoever. When I sell out of all my books an hour before the signing ends, he stands and starts to walk around to the front of the table.

"Where are you going?" I ask.

"You're done," he says. "So am I."

I don't have a chance to respond because more readers approach, and I focus on them. A commotion at the door to the ballroom catches my attention, so I glance in that direction and embarrassment licks my cheeks like white-hot flames.

Rod is animatedly arguing with someone, causing a scene and drawing the attention of almost everyone in the room. I have no clue who he's yelling at, as my boyfriend is blocking them, but it doesn't matter.

I watch with horror as Jamie, Sapphire's husband, races toward Rod, along with several other men. They try to calm him down, but when he continues to shout, two of them grab him by the arms and escort him out, which reveals the target of Rod's temper.

My jaw drops, and my stomach flutters.

Standing in the doorway, staring straight at me, is a face I'd recognize anywhere.

My biker.

Chapter Ten
LEAD

"The jig is up, Prez."

I nod absently at Brew, who's standing slightly behind me as I stare at Nova Stone. I've been hovering outside the ballroom since the book signing started this morning, and my brothers have been taking turns checking on me. I'd be pissed at them for it if I thought their presence was really about me and not based on the fact that each one of them is a horny bastard who wanted to hit on equally horny women.

"You should go talk to her," my Road Captain encourages.

"And say what?"

"I don't know. See if she needs any help or something."

I should listen to him. I want to listen to him. But I don't. Instead, I issue orders.

"Go keep an eye on Rod. He's escalating for some reason, and I don't trust him."

"You got it."

Brew walks away to do my bidding. I breathe a sigh of relief when he doesn't question me because I'm not sure I could explain my concern even if I tried. All I know is the look in Rod's eyes as he was yelling at me was one I've seen on many faces. It was the look of an addict who's running out of their supply. Which makes sense considering when we took out his dealer.

It worries me that there are plenty of people at the resort who could no doubt support Rod's habit, but Rod has proven that he doesn't pay up, and that only leads to trouble. The Black Savages may have lines they won't cross, like killing someone with this many witnesses or taking out our anger on our enemy's friends or family, but that doesn't mean other clubs draw the same lines. Nova could end up hurt, and that's unacceptable.

"Excuse me."

I glance to my right and down at the petite woman who just stepped up next to me.

"Yes?"

"Are you a cover model or something?"

I cough to cover up my laugh. "What?"

"You look like some of the guys on the books in there," she says, pointing into the ballroom.

"I, uh..." I scrub a hand over my face. "No, ma'am. I'm not a cover model."

"But you've got the look." She tips her head at me. "The neck tattoo, the leather vest, all that muscle. I'd do you."

"You'd do..." I shake my head and grin. She can't be a day under sixty-five, and my mind conjures up Mercenary's words from yesterday. *Grannies can get freaky as fuck.* "Definitely not a model. Just a biker."

She narrows her eyes, and the wrinkles in her forehead become more pronounced. I squirm under her scrutiny but refuse to show it. Besides, I'm as flattered as I am weirded out by the whole interaction.

Finally, her face relaxes, and she pats my arm. "It's just as well," she laments. "My hall pass doesn't extend beyond cover models. I think my husband agreed to the whole thing because he knows the chances of me landing a cover model are next to non-existent."

"Hall pass?"

"You know, when a spouse or significant other gives you permission to cheat only under certain circumstances or with a specific person. That's your hall pass. Mine only applies to cover models."

"I see."

No, I don't. Not at all. If I'm with a woman, she's the only woman... no exceptions. And I'm most certainly the only cock she's gonna be handling.

"Anyway, have a good day," she says as she walks into the room, making a beeline for a table where the author is passing out mini bottles of Fireball.

That was... interesting.

I lean against the doorframe and look toward Nova's table. She's returned to interacting with her fans, and she appears to have moved beyond Rod's outburst. Knowing that I can't stand here and stare for the last hour of the event, I move to one of the couches in the common area outside the ballroom.

Pulling out my phone, I resist the urge to open the reading app with Nova's book and instead open my texts and shoot off a quick one to Arrow.

> Me: Rod's looking to score. Can we make that happen?

I try to convince myself that I'm asking in an effort to protect Nova from whatever harm could come to her should he buy from someone else, and I suppose that's part of it. But there's another part of my reasoning, a darker, more savage part: I want to set the fucker up so Nova can see who he really is and then swoop in to 'rescue' her.

I really am a Black Savage.

My phone vibrates with an incoming text.

> Arrow: Should be able to pull together enough to satisfy him.

Don't do it. This isn't the way to make her yours.

> Me: Never mind.

> Arrow: U sure? It'd be easy & a good way to get to him.

I take a deep breath and tap out a reply that will only cause questions I don't want to answer.

> Me: But not a good way to get her.

> Arrow: Prob not… Talked to her yet?

> Me: Fuck off.

I tuck my cell back in my cut, not bothering to wait for another reply. I trust Arrow not to move forward with selling to Rod, even if he sees value in doing so.

The common area starts to fill up as readers funnel out of the ballroom, signaling the end of the signing. Not giving myself time to rethink my actions, I rise from the couch and move in the opposite direction as everyone else: into the ballroom.

My eyes immediately seek out Nova, and she's clearing off her table and packing things into boxes. I weave through the wagons, boxes, and people as I make my way toward her.

"Need some help?" I ask when I reach her table.

Her head whips up, and her eyes widen. "What?"

"Do you need some help?"

"You're the guy from the diner," she says. "Back in Oregon."

"I am." I grin "And you're Nova Stone, author of *Uncaged*."

"How do you know that?"

Fortunately for me, I'm not a total dumbass. I nod toward the tall banner that stands next to her table, using it as the perfect way to keep the fact that I'm reading *Uncaged* to myself. "Says so right there."

She glances at the banner and then back to me. "Oh, yeah. Right."

"I'm Lead, by the way."

"Why are you here?"

"Club business."

I'm wearing my cut, and she writes books about motorcycle clubs, so I know she knows what I'm talking about. It's oddly refreshing to not have to explain myself to her.

Nova looks at my cut, and her eyes shift as she reads the patches. "I've heard about you back home. I know you're one-percenters. So I'm guessing whatever club business brings you here isn't good."

"You could say that."

"And I know you can't tell me what it is."

"True."

She takes a deep breath, then another and another. "I'm sorry Rod was yelling at you."

"Not your apology to make," I tell her honestly. "Besides, I'm used to men like him."

She scrunches her nose. "Men like him?"

Shit.

"Men who like to throw their weight around," I lie. "Comes with the MC life."

"He's not usually like that."

"How many times have you said that in the last twenty-four hours?"

Nova laughs, but there's no humor in it. It doesn't reach her eyes. "More times than I care to count," she admits.

"Hey, Nova," a woman from the table to the left says. "Who's your friend?"

A crimson flush stains Nova's cheeks. "Oh, um..." She looks at me like she has no clue what to say.

"I'm Lead," I tell the woman. "Nova and I are from the same town in Oregon."

The woman whistles. "Why the hell are you with a fuck like Rod when there are men like Lead around?" she asks Nova, then she steps forward and reaches out a hand. "I'm Kristine. It's nice to meet you."

"And I'm Darlene," another woman says as she joins us. "Darlene Tallman."

"I'm Jessa," a third woman says from behind me, forcing me to look over my shoulder. "And this is Rebecca," she adds, pointing to the chick standing next to her.

Nova groans. "And over there is Nikki Landis, KL Myers, DM Earl, and NJ Adel."

I follow her gaze and see four more women staring at me like I have five heads. I'm used to being eye-fucked, but this is different. Their stares are definitely heated, but there's more than lust in their eyes. There's curiosity, almost as if they see me as a research project, an animal to be observed and analyzed in its natural habitat.

"Nice to meet all of you," I say honestly before focusing all my attention on Nova. "And Kristine is right."

"Right?" Nova asks, her forehead wrinkling in confusion.

"You shouldn't be dating a guy like Rod," I clarify.

"I shouldn't be..." Nova shakes her head. "I don't even know you."

"I didn't say you should be dating me," I tell her. "Although that's not the worst idea in the world. Just said you shouldn't be with Rod. He's not—"

I glance at the other women, realizing this isn't a conversation I should be having, let alone in front of such an astute audience. The last thing I need is for my words to end up in print.

"He's not what?" Nova demands, her temper spiking.

The ladies disperse as if they somehow sense that privacy is needed.

"Forget it," I say and move to start gathering items from her table. "Why don't we get you packed up, and I'll help you get all this back to your room?"

Nova crosses her arms over her chest, and her cleavage pillows above the lace trim of her tank. "Finish what you were going to say," she snaps.

Fucking feisty... I like it.

I take a deep breath, giving myself time to come up with anything other than what I was actually going to say. But I can't. Being honest with her isn't giving away club secrets, so there's no reason to hold back.

"Rod's not a good guy," I finally say.

"You don't even know him," she says with a bite in her tone.

"You're right, I don't. But I know his kind."

"His kind?"

"Nova, look, this wasn't my intention when I came in here. I'm not trying to upset you."

"Forgive me if I don't believe you. Now tell me what the fuck you mean by 'his kind'."

She's not going to make this easy. But do I really want her to? If she needs things sugar-coated, then she's not the woman I think she is.

You don't know who she is.

Heaving a sigh, I decide to tell her in no uncertain terms exactly what I mean.

"Nova, you're dating a drug addict who snorts his way to debts he can't pay."

Chapter Eleven
NOVA

"I really am sorry."

I lean against the wall outside the door to my suite and stare at Lead. After he dropped that bombshell on me down in the ballroom, we silently worked in tandem to clean up my remaining swag. He helped me bring it upstairs, and now it's time to face the music.

Face the drug addict, you mean.

Waving dismissively, I force a smile. "It's fine."

"It's not, but than—"

"I should get going," I say as I push off the wall and turn to unlock the door. "We've got dinner plans."

I don't want to talk to Rod about what I've learned, let alone a stranger.

A stranger you've been fantasizing about... a lot.

"Okay, well..." Lead pauses so I look over my shoulder at him. "I'm two suites down if you need anything."

He starts to walk away, clearly getting the hint, but a thought occurs to me that I can't ignore.

"Lead," I say, stopping him in his tracks. He doesn't turn

around, but he makes no move to take another step, so I continue. "Am I in danger?"

It's not like I'm naive. I'm a damn author, and all of my books are centered around one-percenter motorcycle clubs. I can guess what club business the Black Savages are here on, and it's not fucking spring break.

He does turn around now, and my thighs clench at the heated look in his eyes. "Nova, as long as I'm around, you will never be hurt. I promise you that."

With those parting words, he strides the rest of the way to his suite and disappears inside. I might not know the man, but there's no doubt in my mind that he's telling me the truth. I'm safe. As long as Lead is anywhere in the vicinity, I'm safe.

From anything and anyone other than him.

Pushing thoughts of Lead from my mind, I use my key to unlock the door again and shove it open. Rod is sitting on the couch in the living area, and I can't help but look at him with fresh eyes.

When Lead told me Rod is a drug addict, my first thought was to brush it off. Sure, Rod smokes pot occasionally. Hell, so do I. But an addict?

My second thought was to recall how different he's been acting since we left Oregon. Is it because he needs a fix? Is he using more than pot? Or maybe he knew we were being tailed.

My thoughts spiraled from there. And they still are if I'm being honest.

I know Lead didn't confirm that Rod was the 'business' his club is here for, but he didn't have to. It's the only thing that makes sense.

"What took you so long?" Rod asks without looking away from his cell phone.

"Just because you left early doesn't mean I could," I snap

and start to bring everything that was left over inside the room.

"The thing ended a half hour ago," he says unnecessarily. "And I had to pack up."

Rod finally stands from the couch and walks toward me. But he doesn't help. Heaven fucking forbid he lifts a finger to help.

"So, how much money did you make today?" he asks as he crosses his arms over his chest.

On Lead, the move is sexy. On Rod, it's infuriating.

"I don't know. I haven't totaled it all up yet."

"Whatever," he snaps. "I'm hungry. Let's go eat."

I bite my tongue and hold my breath while I count to ten. It doesn't calm me, but it does allow the filter between my brain and my mouth to kick in.

"We've got reservations for seven," I remind him.

"That's an hour from now," he whines.

"So eat a snack or something. Or better yet, go eat by yourself."

I drop the last box onto the floor and let the door slam shut behind me. Pushing past Rod, I walk into the bedroom and somehow manage to refrain from slamming that door too. Not wanting to be near him any longer than necessary, I make quick work of changing into a clean pair of dark wash jeans, a golden-yellow top that hugs my figure, and black knee-high leather boots.

In the bathroom, I scrub my face free of makeup so I can reapply it with a sultrier look. When my eyes are smoky, and my lips are painted a deep crimson, I stare at my reflection in the mirror. I don't know why I'm going to such lengths to look good, especially for a man who doesn't give a shit about me, but that doesn't seem to matter.

Because you're not going to this length for Rod. You're doing it for—

"I'm going to get something to eat," Rod calls through the door. "I'll see ya later."

I rush out of the bathroom and yank open the bedroom door, intent on stopping Rod, but just as I step into the living area, the main door slams. For a split-second, I'm hurt that he left, but then I remember that I'm mad at him and don't want to be around him.

Shrugging off my mood, I decide to make the most of the night. Dinner with friends and colleagues is going to be fun, and I won't have to worry about making profuse apologies like I did last night and today.

And maybe, just maybe, a certain biker will be somewhere close by, making sure I'm kept safe.

"Have a safe trip home."

"I will. It was great seeing you, and I can't wait for the next signing."

Jessa grins. "Same. And who knows, maybe a certain someone will be with you instead of Rod."

I glance over my shoulder in the direction of the lobby entrance where I know Lead is pretending he can't be seen. He's been following us since we left for dinner several hours ago, and I have to admit, it hasn't been awful knowing he's there.

"I doubt it," I say. "Darcie's coming with me as my assistant."

"Didn't say anything about him coming as the help." Her grin widens. "Anyway, I'm heading up to my room. I'm exhausted, and we're heading out early in the morning. Have a good night, Nova."

"You too," I call to her as she steps onto the elevator.

I was going to go to my suite, but I don't feel like it. Not now, not with my shadow so close. I make my way through the back exit of the lobby that leads to one of the resort bars. My heels click against the pavement, and it isn't long before I hear boots thump behind me.

"What are you running from, Nova?"

I stop in my tracks and slowly turn to face Lead. "I don't know," I admit. "You tell me."

"I'm not gonna hurt you."

"Didn't think you were." I tilt my head. "Why have you been following me all night?"

Lead shrugs. "I told you earlier that as long as I'm around, you'd be safe. I'm a man of my word."

"So I've been in danger all night?"

He grins. "No, because I was there."

"Look, I don't know what you're playing at here," I begin. "But I have a boyfriend." When he opens his mouth to speak, I hold a hand up. "I admit, that won't be the case for long, but it's something I have to handle. And I don't need backup to do it."

His eyes darken. "First, I'm not playing at anything. I'm a man, not a boy. I don't fucking play." He takes a deep breath. "Second, you have a boyfriend who's going to get you killed someday if he keeps going down the path he's traveling. And third, I'm not keeping an eye on you because I think you need backup to break up with Rod. I'm keeping an eye on you because Rod has been making the rounds for the last two hours trying to find a fix, and he hasn't been shy about throwing your name out there as the person who will fork over the cash for it."

My stomach bottoms out, and my shoulders sag. "He what?"

"Did I stutter?"

"No."

"Do you really wa—"

Lead's phone rings, and he pauses to answer it with a look of apology. He moves to the edge of the path, and rather than stand around, I continue heading to the bar. He'll find me when he's done.

I pay attention to my surroundings as I walk, but it's dark, and the music from the multiple restaurants and bars at the resort make it difficult to see and hear too much. Several times I glance over my shoulder, but it doesn't take long for Lead to fade into the distance.

I really should've worn my smartwatch to track my steps. This place is fucking huge.

The neon sign comes into view, and my mouth waters thinking about the strawberry daiquiri I'm going to order. Getting caught up in the beat of the music as I get closer, I miss the sound of footsteps behind me.

An arm wraps around me to cover my mouth, silencing my scream, and something hard presses into my back.

"This brings me no amount of pleasure, Darlin'," a man says, and I recognize the voice as belonging to the biker who helped me yesterday. "But club business is club business."

Chapter Twelve

LEAD

I listen to Toot with half an ear as I watch Nova stride down the narrow path toward the bar. Her hips sway, and my cock swells. Fucking hell she's sexy. The second I saw what she'd changed into for dinner, I almost came in my jeans like an inexperienced teenager.

"Are you hearing me?" Toot snaps.

"Huh?" I begin to pace, needing to calm my hormones so I can focus.

"She's in trouble, Prez," he rushes to say. "We've got Rod, but they're coming for Nova."

"Who's coming for Nova?" I demand. "You're not making any fucking sense, T."

He heaves a sigh. "Look, all you need to know is Rod found a hook-up who was willing to deliver a fresh coke supply to his and Nova's suite. Arrow and I were watching him, like you ordered, when Arrow got a call from Fender. Turns out that the dealer Rod was gonna buy from gets his stash from the Soulless Kings chapter in Texas. So Crow, the president of the Texas SKMC—"

"Get to the goddamn point!"

"If you've got eyes on Nova, get her the fuck away from the resort."

I whirl around and race down the path in the direction Nova went. In my effort to focus on what Toot was saying, I lost sight of her.

Rookie mistake, Lead. Rookie fucking mistake.

"Clear out our rooms and theirs and get outta there," I order. "Keep Rod with you, and I'll send a location to meet up once I've secured Nova."

I disconnect the call knowing he'll do exactly as I said. They might not always agree with my orders or understand them, but they always follow them.

Forcing my thoughts to shut down so I can listen for any sound to indicate where she might be, I slow my movements and carefully search every inch of space. When I get closer to the bar, I begin to wonder if I'm overreacting. Maybe she made it and is sitting on a stool and sipping a drink.

I reach the end of the path, but before the entrance to the bar, there's a stretch of pavement that leads to an employee parking lot. The eight-foot gate that keeps resort guests out is closed, but that doesn't mean shit.

A shrill scream from the vicinity of the lot fills the air. With a running start, I launch myself up and over the gate. When I land on the other side, I scan my surroundings and spot movement near the back corner.

"Who's there?" a man asks.

Without answering, I bend to take my knife out of my left boot and the gun out of my right one. Being quiet isn't an option, but I'm counting on the music from the bar to drown out my footsteps. Skirting around several cars, my eyes adapt to security lighting, and I'm able to make out what the movement was. I stay in the shadows as I take in the scene, and my heart splits in two at the frantic look in Nova's eyes.

A man—the one who caused instant jealousy as I watched

him help Nova yesterday—has his arm wrapped around her from behind, and a hand over her mouth. She's struggling against his hold, but her efforts are futile. And aimed at her temple is his gun.

"Show yourself," he demands. "I don't want to hurt her, but I will."

I step out from behind the vehicles and aim my gun at him. "Let her go," I snarl.

"Who the fuck are you?"

Nova's tries to scream, but he only presses his hand more firmly over her mouth, muffling her attempts.

"Your goddamn murderer if you don't let her go."

"Yeah, that's not gonna happen."

I lock eyes with Nova and force myself to soften my expression. "You okay?"

Her chest heaves as she stares at me, and her eyes dart from side to side as if she's trying to figure out how to answer. Finally, she nods.

"Just try to stay calm," I tell her.

Nova tries to nod again, but the man tightens his hold and shakes her.

"Cut the chit-chat," he snaps. "All she has to do is fucking pay me, and we can all walk away from here."

"Pretty sure she doesn't owe you a dime."

He tips his head forward toward me. "You know how this works, brother. I was told to collect my money from her, and that's what I'm doing."

My jaw tics. "I'm not your brother," I snap. "But you're right... I *do* know how this works. You either let her go or get a bullet through your head." I shrug, feigning indifference. "Don't give a fuck which, but either way, Nova walks away from this unscathed."

He leans in and presses his cheek against hers as he lowers his weapon to drag the barrel up her inner thigh.

Nova whimpers as she swivels her hips and flails against him.

"This is your last chance," I grate out. "Let. Her. Go."

I force my eyes to focus on him and not Nova. The fear on her face is gut-wrenching and if I keep my attention on her, I worry I won't be able to act as quickly as I need to.

Taking a deep breath, my vision shrinks to blur out anything and everything but the spot between his eyes. My breathing and heartbeat slow, and a familiar, comfortable calm washes over me.

The world around us disappears, sounds fade, and the trigger calls to me like a Siren calling for her victim.

Nova screams as a bullet pierces her captor's skull, and he slumps to the ground. I relax my hold on my gun and rush forward to make sure she's okay.

"W-what just..." Tears stream down her face as she looks down at the dead man. "You shot him."

"Did you want him to shoot you?"

"You two gotta get the fuck outta here."

I whirl around, shoving Nova behind me as I do. Another biker is standing there with his weapon in his hand, but he's not aiming at us. My eyes dart to the patches on his cut, and the name stitched on one is familiar. Breath whooshes out of me, and the tension leaves my body.

"Crow?" I ask.

"At your service." He glances over his shoulder. "You've got less than two minutes before this place is swarming with cops. Someone had to hear that shot. Go, get outta here and let the Soulless Kings handle things."

Nova leans into my back, and she's shaking. "Do you know him?" she asks.

"No, but I trust him," I answer honestly and reach back to pull her to my side.

She resists at first, but I don't let up. When she's tucked under my arm, I start moving toward the gate.

"Thanks, man," I tell Crow. "And thank Fender for me. No doubt he had a hand in this."

"He wants you to call him when you're safe, so you can thank him yourself."

I nod as I tuck my gun and knife back into my boots. Then I guide Nova out of the parking area. She doesn't struggle, and I have no doubt that shock is taking over, but there's no time to worry about that. Not until we're far from this place.

As we make our way through the resort, I scan our surroundings to make sure we aren't followed. When we reach the main lot, I head straight toward Nova's vehicle.

"Nova, I need your keys," I tell her when we stop next to the passenger door.

She doesn't move to get them as she stares straight ahead. I grab her purse and dig for them myself. When my fingers wrap around the metal keys, I pull them out and unlock the car. I help her into the passenger seat and rush around the front to get in on the driver's side.

After starting the ignition, I shift into gear and peel out of the lot. I consistently check the rearview mirror to ensure we aren't followed, and once I know we're safely away from the resort, I slow to the speed limit and reach across the center console to lift her hand in mine.

"Nova?"

"Hmm?"

"Are you okay?"

I glance at her, but before she can answer, my cell rings.

"What?" I snap as I answer the call.

"You get her?" Arrow barks.

"Yeah, we're heading north in her car." I take a deep breath. "You guys get out?"

"We did." He chuckles. "Rod is currently trussed up in the back, and let me tell ya, he's pissed."

"I don't give a good goddamn if he's pissed," I snap. "What the fuck happened back there, VP?"

Arrow sighs. "Look, let's just all get somewhere safe for the night and then we can talk. Does that work for you, Prez?"

No! I want fucking answers.

But Arrow is right. Talking about this while we're both driving isn't the best use of our time.

"Fine. Put at least sixty miles between us and the resort and find a motel. Nothing fancy. Text me the location when you get there."

"Done."

I disconnect the call and glance at Nova.

"Everything is gonna be fine, Nova," I tell her, trying to inject as much calm into my tone as I can.

I expect her to remain silent, to sit there like a statue, so when she seems to snap out of her shock and twist in her seat to face me, I'm pleasantly surprised.

"No!" she shouts. "No, it's not gonna be fucking fine. Nothing is going to be fine."

I squeeze her hand. "I know it doe—"

"Don't patronize me, Lead," she practically growls. "I'm not some stupid, fragile flower you have to lie to."

Okay. Definitely over the shock.

And absolutely fucking perfect for me.

Chapter Thirteen
NOVA

"Man, he showed up at the perfect time."

I listen with half an ear as I pace the length of the motel room. When we arrived at the Super 8 ten minutes ago, I went straight to the bathroom and locked myself in. I don't know if I was expecting to break down or lose my shit or what, but nothing happened. I stared at my reflection in the mirror for a minute and then... fucking nothing.

"I still don't have all the details, but as soon as I do, I'll let you know."

When I came out of the bathroom, Lead was on the phone. He smiled at me in acknowledgment, but his focus has been on whoever he's talking to.

So I'm pacing.

And waiting.

Not so patiently, I might add. I have so many questions, none of which I got answers to as Lead whisked me away from the resort. Don't think I didn't ask, but he wasn't talking. At least not in any way that didn't continue to come across as patronizing.

Lead chuckles. "Always careful, man. But listen, I've gotta run. We'll chat in a few days."

Stopping to face him, I watch as he disconnects the call. He tosses his cell onto the bed and links his hands behind his head.

"Who was that?" I demand and cross my arms over my chest.

He arches a brow. "A friend."

The whole losing my shit reaction I was expecting earlier barrels out of me like a freight train. I throw my arms in the air and stomp toward Lead, satisfaction sliding through me when his eyes widen slightly.

"I'm only going to say this once, Lead, so you better fucking listen." I stab a finger at his chest and rush to continue before he can interrupt. "I'm not stupid. And I'm not a child. Sugar-coating things with me won't fly. I get that you can't tell me everything because of all that hush-hush, club business bullshit, but that doesn't mean you get to keep secrets that impact me." I take a deep breath. "Especially not when I just watched you kill a man!"

Lead stares at me for a moment, his eyes dark and dangerous. It crosses my mind that maybe, *just maybe*, the fact that I saw him end someone's life so easily should scare me, but it doesn't.

And that scares me.

I back up to put some distance between us, not completely trusting myself to be so close.

"I never said you were stupid, Nova," he finally says. "If you want me to talk to you, to tell you things, then I'm gonna need you to stop putting fucking words in my mouth."

Lead takes a step toward me, and my insides quiver.

What. The. Hell?

"But club business is just that... club business," he continues and takes another step forward. "It has nothing to do with sugar-coating shit or keeping secrets from you. It's about making sure that my club brothers and their families remain safe and protected from any danger the club's dealings might bring to them. The less outsiders know, the safer we all are."

Well, damn.

My shoulders deflate. Research is great for my writing, but apparently, it doesn't take into account one important factor: real, live humans.

People have motivations that can't be found by searching the internet. They can't be ascertained by pouring over website after website about motorcycle club hierarchies, badass biker road names, or ways to get away with murder.

Lead closes the remaining distance between us, and heat radiates from his body. The vein in his neck throbs, causing the lines of his tattoo to ripple. My fingers tingle with the desire to reach out and touch him. But I don't. I can't.

I'm taken.

By a man who threw you to the wolves.

"This is real life, Nova." Lead's voice is low, full of grit. "We're not living in one of your books." I swallow, and I swear I can hear a thunk in my throat. "You can't write away danger or delete the story and start over because you don't like the place you find yourself in. It doesn't work that way."

"Don't you think I know that?" I cry. "I am fully aware that life is messy and doesn't come with do-overs."

Lead's eyes soften as he reaches out and brushes a strand of hair behind my ear. "Real men may let you down, but a book boyfriend never will." He smirks, and I gasp, recognizing the dedication from *Uncaged*, but before I can comment, he continues. "I'm a real goddamn man, Nova, and I won't let you down. But I'm not perfect, and I live a life that's not for everyone. It's unpredictable, exciting, wild, chaotic, and... savage."

My body sways toward him, seemingly without my permission, and Lead's hand slides to my shoulder, holding me away. My eyes snap to his, and embarrassment heats me from the inside out.

Or is that lust?

Either way, I was going to kiss him, and he stopped me. That's humiliating. And right on par with the trajectory of my life at the moment.

"I'm also not a man who kisses a woman who's taken," he says with a sigh. He takes a step back and shoves his hands in his pockets. "Fuck, Nova, I want you. I've wanted you since the moment I saw you in that diner back home. And I've obsessed over you to the point of madness. But just because I cross moral lines that would destroy most people doesn't mean that there aren't any I won't cross. And cheating is one of them."

"I... I'm sorry." I take a deep breath and avert my eyes. "It's just... I don't... Dammit."

"Mark my words, you will be mine, Nova Stone. I will claim you," he growls hotly, and I whip my gaze to lock with his. "But Rod needs to be dealt with first."

"Where is he?" I blurt.

I can't believe it took me this long to even consider my boyfriend, to wonder where he is. But desperate times and all that.

Lead chuckles. "He's in another room with Arrow and Mercenary."

"Arrow," I repeat. "I met him."

"I know. He's my VP."

"And Mercenary?"

"Enforcer."

"Who else is with you?"

Lead moves to sit on the bed, but I remain where I am.

"Brew, Kicker, Brick, and Toot. Road Captain, SAA, and two patched... in that order."

I rub a hand over my forehead, taking in the information he's giving me. It boggles the mind that seven of them came to Texas, and all because of Rod.

"I'd like to see Rod."

"I don't think that's a good idea," he hedges.

"Look, my books might be fiction, but that doesn't mean there aren't some realistic aspects to them. I know Rod has likely been roughed up by your brothers, and I know you're going to ultimately deal with him however you see fit," I admit. "But he's the reason I'm in this mess, and I deserve the chance to confront him about it."

"Nova, I really don—"

"If you want a sliver of a chance in hell of claiming me, you'll let me see him."

Lead stares at me for so long I begin to wonder if he's going to respond at all. Finally, he nods. Pushing up from the bed, he walks to the door.

With his back to me, he says, "Fine, you can see him. But nothing he says or does will change his fate."

"I know."

I follow Lead down the walkway and around the corner to a room on the other side of the building. It's on the tip of my tongue to ask why he didn't demand closer rooms, but I wisely keep my mouth shut. This is his show, not mine. Even if I'm the one most affected by it.

He knocks on the door, and it immediately swings open. Arrow stands there and looks from Lead to me and back again.

"Prez?"

Lead pushes his way inside, and Arrow moves to allow me to pass. The space is small, crowded with so many large men, but it all disappears as my eyes seek out Rod.

He's sitting on one of the two double beds, his back against the headboard. He's not tied up or gagged, but the bruising and swelling on his face tells me he learned the hard way that neither were necessary.

"Can I get a few minutes alone with him?" I ask no one in particular.

"Nope," Lead says matter-of-factly. "I do need to meet with my officers, both here and back at the clubhouse, so I'll be heading back to our room, but Toot and Brick will stay here with you."

I nod, knowing it's the best I'm going to get, but my attention remains on Rod. His eyes are darting around the room, never slowing to stare at any one person. He's sweaty, and I can see his body shaking. I don't know if it's from fear or withdrawal, and I suppose it doesn't matter. He's suffering, and for that, I'm oddly grateful.

"Brick and Toot, if he so much as looks at her wrong, slit his throat."

Rod's eyes widen as far as the swelling will allow, and I have to fight a grin.

"Done, Prez," they say in unison.

The entire exchange is surreal, and would make a perfect scene in one of my books.

And then Lead and his officers are gone, Brick and Toot flank the room, and I'm left to deal with the shithead who landed me in the arms of a man who held a fucking gun to my head.

But I have no clue where to start with Rod, what questions to ask or threats to make. I don't know whether to be pissed off or feel sorry for him. So I start with something else, someone else, in an effort to let my brain and emotions fall into sync.

"So, Toot... that's an interesting road name."

Chapter Fourteen

LEAD

"We're both here, Prez."

My cell sits in the center of the small table, and it's on speaker. Arrow, Brew, Mercenary and I form a circle, while Moose and Shorty are on the other end of the line. I'm not a fan of holding church this way, but it can't be helped. I have no idea who the hell I killed back at the resort, other than he was a biker, which means I don't know if we're going to run into more trouble on the way home.

"What the fuck happened?" I snarl.

"Toot didn't explain it to you?" Arrow asks.

I think back to the brief conversation I had with Toot when he called to tell me Nova was in trouble.

"I know Rod found a score, and that somehow got the Soulless Kings involved. There was exactly time to get into specifics."

"Right," Arrow says. "So, yeah, Rod was looking for more coke. I guess he went through the stash he had from our dealer."

"I figured that out already," I snap. "How did this all end up at Nova's feet?"

I know I need to give them a chance to explain, but I'm not exactly feeling patient at the moment. It's hard to be patient when the only thing I want to do is march back to the other room and drag Nova as far away from Rod as I can manage. I'm not worried about him hurting her, not physically, not with Brick and Toot there. But physical pain is not the only pain he can inflict.

Nova's already been through the emotional ringer. I might not know how or why or who put her through it, but I know it as sure as I know my legal name is Donovan Martin. And the thought of her being subjected to more shit makes me twitchy.

Not to mention the very unwanted worry that she might forgive him for his transgressions. Even if she does, she'll be free because Rod is going to die before this is all over. But the dark, depraved side of me wants her to hate him, needs her to hold onto her rage and let it fuel the rest of her life.

That same part of me knows if she can do that, she's like me. She's my equal in a way that goes beyond rational society's understanding. Because then we're both two black, savage souls bound together by invisible tethers that can't be defined or ignored.

Because then Nova can truly be yours to claim.

"The dealer he made contact with is affiliated with the Banging Bashers MC here in Texas. Local club with no national presence, but hard-core. The Marble Falls chapter of the Soulless Kings is the Bashers supplier, so that's how they got involved," Arrow explains.

"From what we can piece together so far," Moose begins. "Fender's man, Crow, got a call from the Bashers VP asking for a quick delivery. Crow was hesitant because the Bashers owe SKMC a few grand, but when the VP added that the buyer's girlfriend is, and I quote, *rich author, Nova Stone*, and that Nova was who was forking over the cash, Crow agreed."

"If Crow didn't get his money," Mercenary says with a shrug. "No skin off his back. They take out the Bashers, hunt down Nova and blackmail her for their money, and move on."

"In his mind, she's an author, so she's famous. They wouldn't have to physically hurt her." Brew sighs. "So, Crow sent one of his guys to do the exchange, but not long after that, Fender called Crow. Call it fate or luck or whatever, but it's that call that saved Nova's ass."

"How so?"

"Fender called to discuss a prospect that's looking to transfer from Oregon to the Marble Falls chapter," Arrow says. "He also asked for a standard club update, and Crow filled him in on the delivery they were making and how *some famous author* was the end of the line on the deal. Fender put the pieces together and ordered Crow to get to the resort while he called me with the heads up that shit was going to hit the fan."

"It's convoluted, Prez," Shorty says. "Bottom line, things worked out, and everyone is safe."

"Are we though?" I bark. "I killed the Basher's VP. They aren't going to let that go."

"Crow is handling things back at the resort, and Fender assures us that Crow will also handle any fallout with the Bashers," Arrow explains. "Pretty sure the Bashers are coming to a tragic end."

My brothers laugh, but I can't. I don't like this.

"It's not Crow's responsibility to clean up our mess. And that biker's death is on me. I pulled the trigger."

"And it's not our responsibility to clean up Rod's mess," Brew counters quietly. "But isn't that exactly what we're doing, what you did by saving Nova?"

He's right, but I don't like his logic.

"Prez, I think we need to let this one go," Mercenary adds. "Let the Soulless Kings deal with the shit in Texas. I mean, they've got Charlie and Sylvia... don't they owe us for that or some shit?"

"That's not how it works," I snap. I take a deep breath. "Fine, we'll let them handle it. But we'll owe them one... I think. I've lost count over the years."

"That's between you and Fender," Arrow says.

"I hate to bring this back to more immediate issues," Moose starts. "But what now?"

"Now we take the rest of the night and get some rest," I say. "We'll hit the road in the morning, and we drive until we reach the clubhouse. The only stop we make is to pick up our bikes in Twin Falls. Crow and his crew might be willing to deal with the Bashers, but that doesn't mean we won't run into trouble. We don't know who the Bashers have as allies or if any of them will break away before the Soulless Kings attack."

"What about Rod and Nova?" Brew asks.

"What about them?"

"Is Rod making it back to Oregon?"

"No." I heave a sigh. "I'll ask Fender for one more favor and see if we can dispose of him in Twin Falls. We'll kill him between here and there. When he was simply a junkie who owed us money, Rod had a chance. But the second he put Nova's life in jeopardy, any hope he had fizzled to nothing."

"And Nova?" Arrow asks with a smirk.

"She's mine," I say without hesitation. "Touch her and you'll end up buried in Twin Falls with Rod."

"Wasn't planning on touching her, Prez," Arrow drawls. "I was just wondering where your head was at."

"Nova's mine," I repeat, in case it wasn't clear the first time. "As for what happens when we get back to Oregon... stay tuned." Heat rolls through me at the thought of what will transpire between Nova and me when we get home.

Things... dark, dirty things. "All in favor of letting Crow handle all things Texas, say 'aye'."

"Aye," is said in unison.

"All in favor of eliminating Rod, say 'aye'."

Same response.

"Good," I say. "Now let's get some fucking sleep."

The call is disconnected, and I grab my cell to shove it in my pocket. I move to the door but hesitate when the hairs on the back of my neck stand on end. I slowly turn to face my brothers.

"What?" I bark.

Mercenary takes a step back, Brew raises his hands as if surrendering, and then there's Arrow. Fucking Arrow.

My VP grins. "Where's Nova gonna sleep tonight, Prez?"

I point to the bed closest to the bathroom. "Right fucking there. Got a problem with it?"

"Nope, no problem." His grin widens. "Where are you gonna sleep, Prez?"

I stalk toward him and wrap my hand around his throat. "I'm gonna sleep as close to her as she'll fucking let me," I snarl.

"And if she doesn't want to share a room with you?" Mercenary asks, suddenly not so concerned about my wrath.

I shove Arrow away from me and return to the door. "I'm going to the other room. I suggest you unload the vehicles so we all have shit to change into." I yank the door open. "Oh, and make sure you bring Nova's laptop in," I tack on, thinking that writing may help her relax. It's her job, so who knows, but mayhem and chaos is my job, and it relaxes me. "Meet me back in your room when you're done."

With that, I leave them to do my bidding. My heart thuds in my chest as I walk toward the room where Nova is with Rod. The closer I get, the more my annoyance wanes and nerves take over.

It's not nerves, jackass.

I assess what I'm feeling, how my body is reacting to her growing nearness. And I realize my subconscious is right. It's not nerves. Nova doesn't make me nervous.

It's excitement.

She excites me on a level I didn't even know was possible.

Chapter Fifteen
NOVA

"Babe, I'm sorry."

I roll my eyes at Rod. It's the fourth time he's apologized, but he hasn't been sincere even once. He's not sorry I could've been hurt. He's sorry he got caught. He's sorry that he's craving whatever shit he's used to having in his system but doesn't.

"Cut the shit," I snap. "I'm not your babe. Fuck, I'm not your anything anymore."

For the first time since we started talking, he seems genuinely panicked. I'm not naive enough to believe that it's because he doesn't want to lose me, but the panic is real. I'm guessing it's because he was counting on me to save him and is only now realizing that's not likely to happen.

Rod scrambles to the foot of the bed, and Toot and Kicker move toward him, but I hold up a hand to stop them.

"He's fine," I tell the two bikers, and they stop. If Rod means me real harm, they can easily get to him but for now, I can handle him.

"Babe, please," Rod pleads. "You gotta believe me. I love you, and would never do an—"

Thwack!

My palm stings when it connects with Rod's cheek.

"Dayum," Toot says with admiration.

"Nothing shrinks a man's balls faster than being bitch-slapped by a pint-sized spitfire," Kicker adds with a chuckle. "I do not envy you, Rod. Not at all."

"I don't believe a word that comes out of your mouth," I snarl. "You say you love me like it means something, like it's a truth that will fix everything. It's like you don't know me at all."

"But I do love you," he insists.

"Ya know what? Maybe you do. In some twisted, fucked up way, I think you do love me. But that doesn't mean you wouldn't hurt me." I inhale deeply to reign in my emotions. "Love is a damn illusion, Rod. It's a word people throw around when it suits them, when they think the situation calls for it. Love isn't a shield against pain, it's not a magical pill one can swallow to make them a good person. It's fictional, and it's fleeting."

"Lead is so fucked," Kicker mutters.

Ignoring him, I remain intensely focused on the man who I allowed to take too much of my time and energy.

"So yeah, Rod, you love me. Because it suits you. Because it makes you feel better. But in the end, it didn't matter because you still sent that goon after me, you still sacrificed me to save yourself."

"But you're okay, Nova. You weren't hurt, not really."

"Maybe not this time, but what about the next? And the time after that?" I ask, but I don't give him a chance to respond. "You will never change. And quite frankly, I don't give a damn. Because you're not my problem anymore. The difference between us, Rod, is that I went into this relationship with my eyes wide open. I knew from day one that it would never amount to anything because permanence, like love, doesn't exist. I knew that we'd end at some point. But I don't think you did. I don't think you heard a word I ever said about my thoughts on marriage and relationships, and you thought I'd be a meal ticket for the rest of your miserable life. Well..." I shrug. "Joke's on you, isn't it?"

"Tell him, bitch," Toot cheers. I glare at him, and he smiles sheepishly. "Sorry... Nova."

A knock on the door draws my attention. My chest heaves from my rant, but for the first time since I don't know when, I feel lighter, happier... right.

Kicker opens the door, and Lead strides in. He immediately comes to my side and levels his gaze on me.

"You okay?"

I smile. "I'm great."

"Are you about done here?"

I glance at Rod, who's glaring at me and Lead.

"Almost," I tell Lead.

"Are you kidding me?" Rod snaps. "You're fucking him, aren't you?"

Lead moves toward Rod, but I lunge faster and land a punch to Rod's face. His head whips to the side and bounces back. Pain radiates through my hand, but the way his eyes water and blood trickles from his nose makes it worth it.

I get it now... the satisfaction that my heroines feel when they stand up for themselves.

"I haven't fucked him," I say from behind clenched teeth. I lean forward and get as close to Rod's face as I can without it being intimate. "But who knows? Maybe that'll change. I certainly don't have to worry that anything I do with Lead can be seen as cheating because you and I are over."

I straighten and turn to face Lead. He's watching me with heat and respect in his eyes, and my panties dampen. His nostrils flare, and the muscles under his shirt tense.

Yep. Good thing I'm now a single woman because I'm so gonna fuck this man.

Over and over and over.

"Now I'm done," I say and move to stand in front of Lead. I'm so close I can touch him, flatten my palms on his chest and jump up into his arms, but I don't.

"So that's it?" Rod asks, unable to accept anything I've said to him. "You're dumping me? You're leaving me with them to do... whatever it is that they do?"

I glance over my shoulder and smile sweetly. "How's it feel to be thrown to the wolves?"

Without waiting for a response, I step around Lead and walk to the door. "You coming?" I call over my shoulder.

"Lock that shit down, Prez."

"She's club queen material."

"Not yet."

All three of them speak at once, but the only statement I focus on is Lead's.

Not yet.

I pull open the door and duck when Arrow's fist almost collides with my forehead as he was preparing to knock.

"Damn, sorry, Nova," Arrow says sheepishly as he steps around me into the room. "So, what'd we miss?"

Brew and Mercenary are now in front of me, making no move to pass like Arrow did. With a laugh, I respond to Arrow.

"So damn much, VP," I say without turning around. Then I slap Mercenary and Brew on their chests. "Do your worst boys. And please, have fun."

I start down the walkway, chuckling as I hear questions being rapid fired at Lead. He orders them to hold off on killing Rod until we get to a more remote area, and then the distinct sound of boots thudding against concrete reach my ears.

"Wait up," Lead calls from behind me.
"Hurry up," I reply, smiling to myself.

Chapter Sixteen
LEAD

"So, um..."

The confident, feisty woman from five minutes ago is gone, and in her place is a shy, timid Nova. She's standing at the foot of the bed closest to the bathroom, the one I told my brothers I'd be sleeping in with her if she let me. And because they always have my back, the other bed is covered with several bags.

Not that they can't be thrown to the floor if the bed is needed.

"What now?" she asks, looking everywhere in the room but at me.

As soon as I unlocked the door and she crossed the threshold, she shifted. At first, I wondered if she was just putting on a show for Rod, but then she turned to face me, and I saw the blush on her cheeks and heat in her eyes. She isn't second-guessing shit. But she's also not going to take the lead.

I take tentative steps toward her, as if moving too fast will spook her.

"Look at me, Nova," I command. She does for the briefest of seconds, but then she lowers her head. "Look. At. Me."

Nova hesitates, but then she takes a deep breath and lifts her head. Her eyes lock on mine, and she pulls her bottom lip between her teeth.

And I'm a goner. My cock swells beneath my jeans, and my heart races in my chest. As for Nova, her breathing is shallow, and the pulse-point at her throat throbs.

As much as I want to throw her on the bed and devour her like a starving man, I recognize that addressing a few things might help her relax.

"First of all, are you okay?" I ask.

Her forehead wrinkles with confusion. "Why wouldn't I be?" she retorts earnestly.

"Oh, I don't know. It's been a crazy few hours, for starters."

"Oh. Yeah, I'm fine. A mini kidnapping won't break me."

I chuckle at her description. "Noted. But that won't happen again."

She nods.

"And you're okay with the whole Rod thing?"

"What, with breaking up with him?"

"That," I confirm. "And knowing he's going to die."

She asked me not to sugarcoat things so I'm not.

Nova seems to think about my words, and then she nods succinctly. "Yeah. I'm good." She shrugs. "I mean, I'm not all 'yay, un-aliving', but I—"

"Un-aliving?"

"Yeah, sorry. It's a term that a lot of authors use on social media in place of 'murder'. 'Murder' triggers bots, and that can land us in hot water with the social media police so that's our workaround," she explains.

"There is so much I don't know."

"Join the club," she says with a humorless chuckle. "Anyway, I may not be a big supporter of killing people, but I get it. I know how things work with an MC. He fucked up, and now there are consequences. I may have given your guys the green light, but his death is on him, not me."

"Wow. That's, uh..." I search for the words but find none.

"Realistic," she finishes for me.

"Something like that."

"Look, I know I may seem cold-hearted, but everything I said to Rod was the truth," she says, seemingly forgetting that I wasn't present for whatever she did or didn't say to him. I open my mouth to ask her about it, but she continues. "Love doesn't exist. I wasn't looking for sunshine, rainbows, and happy endings with him. It was never going to be forever. It is what it is."

Her short, jaded explanation saddens me, which is odd because until I met her, I thought the exact same things about love. I'm not saying I love her, because I don't know, but I'm more willing to open myself up to the possibility that I was wrong, and it does exist.

"Is talking about love really what you want to be doing right now?" she asks.

"I want to make sure you're okay," I reply. "And when we fuck, I wanna know it's because it's what you really want and not some high your riding because the stories in your head are jumping out into reality."

Nova sits on the edge of the bed. "Lead, if I sleep with someone, I promise you, it's because I want to. I'm just feeling a bit..."

I sit next to her. "A bit what?"

Nova turns to look at me, and if I'm not mistaken, it's shame that's in her eyes. "Alive," she breathes. And once the word is out, the shame disappears and is replaced by a light. "For the first time in so fucking long, I feel alive, Lead. I feel like I've been living half a life up until now. I daydream, I write, and I repeat. Daydream, write, repeat. Don't get me wrong, I wouldn't trade being an author for anything in the world. I love it more than I ever thought I would. But my books are not my life. And if I'm being honest, there's a part of me that wishes they were."

"So is that what this is?" I ask, waving my hand between us. "You wanting to live out your fantasies? Is this just research?"

"No," she cries as she shakes her head. "No, Lead, that's not what this is." Nova takes a deep breath and tries to explain. "This is me admitting that my reality isn't reality at all. It's just another story I tell people because I don't know how to be who I want to be, who I am deep down in the depths of my soul."

"And who do you want to be?"

"I wanna be Nova fucking Stone, MC romance author, and badass bitch. I wanna be fun and dark and raw and powerful and real." She flattens her palm against my chest. "I wanna be the woman I am when I'm around you. I wanna be... me."

I rise from the bed and pull her up with me. She eyes me with curiosity but remains quiet.

I strip out of my cut and turn to hang it over the chair behind me in the corner. Next, I reach back and pull my shirt over my head, baring my chest and tattoos to her. After dropping it to the floor, I unbutton my jeans.

Nova's sharp intake of breath is like music to my ears, but it's her fingers stopping my movements that level me.

"Let me," she says as she tugs my zipper down.

Nova pushes the denim over my hips, taking my boxer briefs with them. I kick off my boots, toe off my socks, and free my legs of clothing. Nova's eyes are fixed on my dick, which is standing proudly at attention... for her. Only for her.

And then she giggles. Actually fucking giggles.

"What's so funny?" I snap.

She lifts her eyes to mine and shakes her head. "It's just... I... I write sex scenes for a living," she says, throwing her arms up in the air. "And they can be so cliché, but they're hot, and now that I have you naked, I'm..."

"You're what?"

"I'm wondering if the things I write are even possible."

I grin wickedly as the first sex scene in the book I'm reading pops into my head, and satisfaction slithers through me at the knowledge that she hasn't experienced everything she's dreamed of. I get to show her, teach her, worship her.

Reaching out, I slide my hands up her shirt and cup her tits through her lace bra.

"Oh yeah, like what things?" I ask as I pull the cups of her bra down and run my thumbs over her nipples.

Nova drops her head back and moans. "Like, uh, um..." When I pinch her nipples, she whimpers. "Multiple O's, squirting..."

I unclasp her bra before taking her shirt and it off, exposing her to me. "What else?" I ask as I bend over and lick a path down her stomach.

"Uh, well, getting off on cock alone, praise kinks, anal sex feeling good..."

I take off her boots, and then strip her free of her jeans and panties. Leaning forward, I bury my nose in her pussy and inhale the scent of her arousal.

"What else?" I ask against her clit, savoring the way she trembles.

"There is, um... there is this one thing I'd like to try," she admits. I flick her clit with my tongue once and then stand to look her in the eyes. I nod for her to continue. "Getting tongue fucked while being held upside down against a wall."

"Like Jefferson did to Stacy in *Uncaged?*"

Her eyes widen, and her pupils dilate. "Yeah."

I think about the logistics for a second, desperately wanting to make this happen. Not only for her, but fuck, the scene was hot as hell and immediately went into my spank bank. To make it reality is...

I shudder.

"Can you do a handstand?"

She nods.

"Then what are you waiting for?"

Nova turns toward the wall and kicks herself into a handstand, so her back is against the wall. She's a little wobbly on her arms, so I move to lift her up, and within seconds, her pussy is at mouth level, the perfect level, and her hanging hair tickles my thighs.

"Spread your legs," I demand.

Nova complies but makes a demand of her own. "Spread yours."

When I widen my stance, she wraps one hand around my cock and the other around my hip to grip my ass cheek. Lowering my head, I swipe my tongue through her folds. Her taste bursts in my mouth, and I groan.

"Fucking hell," I mutter against her.

I switch my focus to her clit, knowing that, for this to work, I'm gonna need to make her come fast. With her hand on me, her face so close to my cock, I won't be able to remain upright for long.

Alternating between flicks, licks, and sucks, I work her bundle of nerves until Nova's is a quivering mass of bliss in my arms. She pumps my dick, but there's little rhythm in her movements. Some men might give a damn about that, but I'm not some men. The fact that she can't concentrate tells me that I'm doing my job well.

And what a job it is. If I could get paid to eat Nova's pussy, I'd never fucking retire. Hell, I don't even need paid. I just want the chance to do it for the rest of my days.

Nova's grip tightens, and her nails dig into my ass as her knees bend and her legs drop. I increase the pace of my tongue and within seconds, she comes apart. I don't let up until her body relaxes, and she drops her arms.

I keep my arms around her and move to the bed. Sitting on the mattress, I keep to the very edge so her head can hang over.

"Do you need a break?" I ask her, needing to know she's not going to pass out if she remains upside down a little while longer.

Rather than answer, she does exactly what I had in mind and wraps her lips around my cock.

"Aw, shit," I groan.

Nova's body shifts, and I realize she's braced herself with her hands on the floor, but I still don't let go. I couldn't even if I wanted to. Not when she's deep-throating me like a champ.

She pulls back to swirl her tongue around my head and then bobs her head back and forth, back and forth.

"Take that cock like a good girl," I demand. Nova hums around my length. "That's it. Such a good girl."

I want to thrust my hips, fuck her mouth so my balls slap against her face, but I don't have enough leverage. So instead, I sit here, coiled so fucking tight, as she sucks me off. The tip of my cock hits the back of her throat, and Nova stills before she swallows, the motion sending me into oblivion.

My cum coats her throat, and Nova backs off, but she doesn't stop, she doesn't release me. She continues to suck and swirl and lick until my orgasm renders me helpless. Nova licks me clean and wiggles for me to release her.

When I do, she lowers herself to the floor. My eyes are

closed, but I feel her shift so she's facing me, and then she taps me on the thigh.

I open my eyes to look at her, and fuck me, she swallows before darting that pink tongue out to lick my cum off her lips.

"Good fucking girl."

Chapter Seventeen
NOVA

Scene from *Uncaged?* Check.

Praise kink unlocked? Check.

"You're a squirter," Lead says before licking his lips.

Squirting? Check.

But there are still a few more things on my 'does it happen' list. I rise to my feet and straddle him. Lead wraps his arms around my waist and stands before turning around and practically tossing me onto the mattress.

Rather than join me, he stands and stares, his gaze like a physical caress as he slides it from my face, all the way down to my toes and back again.

"You are stunning," he grits. "Absolutely, sinfully stunning."

I'm usually uncomfortable with compliments, but with Lead, nothing feels uncomfortable. Instead, every second, every word, every action feels… right.

"You're the devilish embodiment of a Greek god."

Lead grins as he tugs on his hard cock. "I've been called a lot of things, but that has to be my favorite."

"I'm sure I can do better, but my brain is mush." I shrug.

He rests his knees on the bed and crawls up my body, his dick still in his hand. "You can't possibly improve on perfection."

When he leans over me, I grab his face and pull him forward, fusing my lips to his. He moves his arms to either side of my head to brace himself on his elbows.

He teases the seam of my lips, and I open for him, our tongues dueling for dominance. Lead's fingers absently play with my hair, and he lowers his body to align it over mine. My nipples graze his chest, and his cock presses into the apex of my thighs.

Lead breaks the kiss and shifts to my neck where he nibbles for a moment before moving to my ear.

"I'm gonna fuck you, Nova Stone," he growls as he moves in between my legs, spreading them as wide as he can. "I can smell how ready you are for me." He grinds his hips. "Can you feel how ready I am for you?"

I nod.

The head of his cock nudges at my entrance, and I release a sigh of pleasure. I grab his hips and pull him toward me, and taking the hint, Lead thrusts into me in one long, smooth stroke.

"Aahhhh," I moan huskily.

"Wrap your legs around me," he demands, and like the good girl he called me earlier, I obey without hesitation.

And then Lead fucks me like the dirty girl I want to be.

I lift my hips to meet his thrusts, and his thick cock drags along my inner walls. With each deep impale, he hits a spot inside of me that I've read about, I've written about, but never experienced. The G-spot.

It exists!

As he pistons in and out, in and out, he leans forward and traps a nipple between his teeth. He lightly nibbles and then rolls the peak between his lips while he flicks it with the tip of his tongue. The sensation is exquisite torture and increases the pleasure building from the inside out.

Lead expertly plays my pussy like it's an instrument created solely for him. Alternating between long, hard thrusts and slow, teasing strokes, he brings me to the edge of bliss. Over and over again he takes me to the brink of shattering, only to switch his rhythm.

Shifting back to my ear, he whispers, "Are you ready to come for me?"

I nod.

"Words, Nova. Use your words."

"Make me come, Lead," I plead. "Please make me come."

"Good." He licks the shell of my ear. "Girl."

He pounds into my pussy, setting an unrelenting pace and hitting that magical spot with each thrust. On every draw back, his pelvis drags along my clit. My vision starts to darken, and the pressure builds.

"Come for me," he growls, and I swear I leave my body as the most intense orgasm tears through me.

I spasm around him, and several strokes is all it takes for his body to tense and his cock to pulse with his release.

As I slowly fall back down to Earth, my limbs shake. I think we're done, but Lead shows me how mistaken I am. He pulls out and slides down my body, latching onto my clit and assaulting it with his tongue.

"Oh shit," I say with a moan as he teases the sensitive bundle of nerves. "I can't. I can't take any more."

"You can," he growls against my throbbing pussy. "You can, and you will."

Lead shoves two fingers inside of me and scissors them as he traces lazy circles around my clit. When he sucks the nub into his mouth and flattens his tongue on it, he finger fucks me. I thought I couldn't take any more, but he's proving me wrong as he quickly brings me to another orgasm.

This time, when my body trembles and quivers with aftershocks, he releases me. Scooting back up and bracing himself on his elbows again, he presses a soft, wet kiss to my lips, letting me taste myself on him.

Orgasm with cock alone? Check.

Multiple Os? Check, check, and check.

"I know there's one more item on your list," he says as if somehow sensing that I'm mentally checking items off. "But I don't have lube, and I refuse to hurt you."

"I think I can wait for that one," I admit. "But I may come up with more for that list."

"If you dream it up, we'll try it."

Lead presses a quick kiss to my lips before rolling to the side and tucking me into the crook of his arm. We lay there for a while, and the only sound penetrating my post-bliss fog is the thumping of his heartbeat when I shift to rest my head on his chest.

My mind races as I recall the last few days. I don't know how I went from dating a prick to fucking the real-life version of one of my heroes, but I'm not complaining.

If I'm being honest with myself, ditching Rod was going to happen with or without everything else that happened before we left the resort. He wasn't the man for me, despite how hard I tried to make him fit into that box. Live and learn, right?

I don't know if Lead and I would've met under different circumstances, but there's no sense trying to wonder about that. We met. A world where we don't doesn't exist.

But still... there is the diner back home so maybe we would have.

I don't believe in fairy tales, and I never will. But I'm starting to wonder if there aren't other possibilities, other connections that are even better than fairy tales because they allow a person to be their true self.

And damned if I don't want to see if those possibilities exist for Lead and me outside of this weekend.

"What're ya thinking?" he asks as he lazily strokes his fingers over my back.

"Nothing," I lie.

"Bullshit," he says with a laugh. "You're a writer. I doubt there's a time where you're ever not thinking."

"I don't know," I tease. "I wasn't thinking much a few minutes ago."

"You know what I mean."

I sigh. "Yeah, I do."

"So?" he prods.

Taking a deep breath, I debate on what to tell him, and I settle on the truth... sort of.

"Possibilities."

"I can't believe you wouldn't let me into the shower with you."

I glance at Lead, who's pouting in the passenger seat as I drive for an hour or two. We stopped to eat a few minutes ago, and I suggested he let me drive while I could since he's already told me that he'll want to be the one to get us through the gate of the Soulless Kings clubhouse in Twin Falls. I don't know if that's a biker thing or what, but it doesn't really matter.

"We had twenty minutes before we had to check out," I remind him.

"So. I'd have had you coming in two."

"But I'd already come three times this morning."

"So?"

"You're insatiable."

"And you're not, miss 'make me come one more time,

Lead'?"

"Are you complaining?" I counter.

"As long as your riding my face or my cock, I'll never complain."

I huff out a breath. "If it makes you feel any better, I came up with another item for my list while I was showering."

"Oh yeah?"

"Uh huh."

"Are you going to tell me what it is?"

"Nope," I say, popping the P.

"Aw, c'mon."

"Fine. It involves your bike."

"Tell me more," he demands.

"It might also require a remote and incredi—"

My phone rings, and Lead groans at the interruption. Thinking it might be Darcie since I haven't talked to her in two days, I hand the cell to him.

"Put it on speaker for me, will ya?"

He does, and I instantly regret it.

"Novalyn Stone, why the hell haven't you been answering my texts?"

I slide my eyes from the road to Lead and see his curiosity is piqued.

"Hi, Mom."

"That's not an answer," she snaps. "You couldn't be bothered to show up for my wedding yesterday, and now your ignoring my texts. I raised you better than that."

"I'm not rehashing why I wasn't there," I tell her. "As for the texts, I'm sorry. I've been busy."

And that's the truth. I have been busy. But I did see the dozen text notifications when I woke up this morning and chose not to respond.

"Apology accepted." Her tone does not match her words.

"When can you come for a visit? I'd like you to meet your stepdad."

"I don't know," I say as I roll my eyes. "I've got a few more signings over the next couple of months, and several deadlines."

She huffs. "Fine. When can we come visit you?"

Shit.

"I, um... Mom, I don't know when a good time would be. But I can call you once I'm home and can look at my schedule."

"How about the week after next?" she asks as if I hadn't spoken. "We can come after the honeymoon. He's taking me to Aruba, Novalyn," she says with excitement. "Did I tell you that? Did I tell you he's taking me to Aruba?"

"No, Mom, you didn't."

"Well, he is. We fly out tomorrow."

"That'll be fun."

"Did you tell your dad that I was getting married?" she asks, and there's a tinge of sadness in her tone, a tinge I haven't heard in a long time.

"No. Was I supposed to?"

"Oh, no. I was just curious." She takes a deep breath. "Well, I gotta run. But I'll call you when we get home and finalize the details of our visit. Love you!"

She disconnects the call before I can protest.

"Fuck!" I shout as I pound the steering wheel, setting off a quick beep of the horn.

"Did you seriously skip your mother's wedding?" Lead asks incredulously.

"You would've too if you knew her," I snap. "She's a habitual bride-to-be."

"Hey, no judgment. Just... I guess that phone call fills in a few gaps for me."

"Oh? What gaps?"

"Your aversion to love and fairy tales."

"That started years ago, when my dad left."

"I'm sorry."

I shrug. "It's fine."

"It's not, Nova. It clearly hurt you. Still does if I had to guess."

I snort. "It doesn't still hurt. But yeah, at the time, it was like someone ripped my heart out of my chest and altered it so it wouldn't fit quite right when it was put back."

"Real men may let you down, but book boyfriends never will," he says, throwing my own words back at me. "Not all men are your dad."

Lead threads his fingers through my hair at the back of my head and massages. It feels heavenly and relaxes my frayed nerves.

"I'm not your dad."

"I know."

"And I'm not Rod."

"I definitely know."

"And I won't let you down."

"I want to believe that."

"What's holding you back?"

"Experience."

"Then I guess I'm gonna have to prove it to you."

"How do you plan on doing that?"

"Oh, Nova. That's simple. I prove that I'm not going to let you down by not letting you down."

It is simple. And yet, so very complicated.

Possibilities, Novalyn. Focus on the possibilities.

Chapter Eighteen
LEAD

"I wanna come with you."

I narrow my eyes at Nova. We arrived at the Soulless Kings clubhouse in Twin Falls almost an hour ago, and Rod has been stashed in their Nightmare Room since then. We decided to wait until we got here to eliminate him just to be safe. No sense carting around a corpse if we don't have to.

"Nova, that's not gonna happen."

"It's fine with me, if that's the concern," Sarge, the Twin Falls chapter president says, and I glare at him. "What? Seems to me she's earned the right to be a part of this after what he set her up for."

"That wasn't my concern," I bark, forgetting for a moment that I'm on his turf, not mine.

Sarge has no problem reminding me though. "Listen, Lead, I'm doing you a favor. I could make you transport that piece of shit all the way back to Oregon. My club, my home, my rules. If I say she can go, she can go."

I take several deep breaths to keep from lashing out again. I already owe the Soulless Kings several favors at this point, no need to rack up more.

"Fine." I look at Nova. "Under one condition."

"What's that?"

"I take his life. I don't want that darkness to touch you."

"No."

"Excuse me?"

"You heard me," she snaps. "No. I'm not saying it won't be you, but I won't promise that it will be."

"Jesus, I should've sent you with the others."

Arrow and Mercenary are the only two of my brothers who are still here, as I sent Brew, Kicker, Toot, and Brick on their way as soon as we arrived. We've been gone long enough, and business back home needs taken care of.

"And that would've been a big mistake, as I pointed out when you tried," she reminds me.

"Threatening to never see me again was pointless and you know it," I retort. "Sure, you probably could stay away for a few days, but you'd miss me at some point."

"Whatever. Just get over your macho bullshit. I'm going with you, and that's that."

"Nova, I don't wa—"

"Sarge," she says and faces him. "Can you take me to this Nightmare Room? If he's not gonna get on board, then I'll go without him."

"I can, but I won't. I have no problem backing you on this and insisting you be allowed to go, but taking you without him?" Sarge shakes his head. "Not gonna happen."

"Nova, if you'd ju—"

"No!" she shouts, and all eyes turn toward us. We're standing in the middle of their common room, and so far everyone has left us alone. But I'm afraid that's coming to an end real fast. "I am not fragile, Lead. I won't fucking break. You want to keep that darkness away from me, and I want to embrace it." Her chest heaves as she lashes out. "If you want this to work, if there's going to be anything good between us, you have to let me embrace it."

"She's right, Prez."

I whip my head to glare at Arrow, who's now joined us. "Stay out of it."

"Can't do that, Prez," he says. "She's right, and you know it. You're a fucking Black Savage. The club's name says it all. And if ever there's a woman who can stand at your side as queen, it's Nova. But not if you don't give her the chance. I get it, brother. You want her to stay light, clean, *good*. And she is all those things. But there are two sides to every fucking coin, my man. You're dark, she's light. You're bad, she's good. And on the flip side of that, she's dark, and you're light. She's bad, you're good. You balance each other out. Embrace that."

"When the hell did you become so philosophical and wise?" I snap.

He shrugs. "Two sides to every coin, Prez. Two goddamn sides."

My VP walks away, and Nova stares at me expectantly.

"So?" she asks. "What's it gonna be?"

I heave a sigh. "Let's go."

Nova launches herself at me and slams her mouth over mine as I lift her into my arms. I dart my tongue between her lips and kiss the fucking hell out of her.

"As heartwarming as this is, I've got shit to do," Sarge says, and I set Nova back on her feet. He points to a hallway off the common room. "Down that hall, steel door at the end. Four three two eight is the code at each entry point." When I stare at him, he smirks. "We change it daily," he says dryly. "Nightmare Room is downstairs. Can't miss it."

"Thanks, Sarge," I say as I shake his hand. "Appreciate it."

"I'd say any time, but you've been exhausting."

He walks away, and I lead Nova down to the room where Rod is being held. The Black Savages has our own version of a torture chamber, but it's not as fancy. It gets the job done, and that's all I care about. I'd rather spend my resources elsewhere anyway.

"You sure about this?" I ask before opening the door to the room. "Once we're inside, there's no backing out."

"I'm sure," she says without hesitation.

I bend down and grab my gun and knife out of my boots. When I hand the knife to her, she arches a brow.

"You want to be a part of this, then you're a part of this. All in. But mark my words, Nova. This won't be a regular occurrence."

"I understand."

I nod curtly. "Good." I cup her cheek. "It's not because I don't think you can handle it. It's because you shouldn't have to."

"Okay."

"Ready?"

"Absolutely."

Her lips tip into a grin, and I swear it's as savage as mine.

I enter the security code, and the door slides open. Once we step inside the room, it closes behind us with a sharp click.

"Oh, Nova, thank God," Rod says with relief. "I knew you'd come get me."

Nova tilts her head. "You did? I thought I made it pretty clear that we're over."

Rod Adam's apple bobs as he swallows. "Well, yeah, you did, but I was hoping... Surely you've had a change of heart."

"Oh, she's had—"

Nova holds a hand up, and I press my lips together. When the hell I became a man who let a woman control the room, I don't know, but not gonna lie... it's fucking hot to watch.

She strides toward Rod, who's strung up in the middle of the room by a chain.

"Ya know what, Rod?" She pauses, giving the illusion that she wants an answer, and when he opens his mouth to speak, she continues. "I did have a change of heart." The hope in his eyes is unmistakable, and I love it. "But not about you. We *are* done."

"Th-then what?" he stammers.

"I think I might just believe that love is real," she admits. "Oh, not the fairy-tale kind. No sunshine and rainbows for this chick." She taps the blade against her chest. "But the kind that I write about? The kind where a real man makes me feel things I thought I was numb to? Yeah, I just might believe in that."

"B-but I lo—"

"Oh, and one more thing," she says. "Remember when you asked if I was fucking him?"

He nods.

Her hand tightens around the knife. It's a subtle movement at her side, but I catch it. Rod, however, does not.

Poor bastard.

"Well," she begins as she thrusts the blade into his stomach. She twists her wrist, and he screams the gargled, bloody scream of a dying man. "I am."

So. Fucking. Hot.

EPILOGUE

Nova

One year later...

"Everything is packed and ready to go."

I grin at Lead. We're heading to Motorcycles, Mobsters, and Mayhem in Texas for the signing this weekend, and this time around, I didn't have to get ready alone. Darcie is coming too and should be here in about thirty minutes.

And bonus, I didn't have to beg off another wedding. My mom's marriage seems to be sticking... for now. She didn't visit the week she said she was going to, mostly because I ignored her calls for a while, but when the new husband called and asked me to visit them, I relented. He was so damn nice, it was impossible to say no.

"Thank you."

"Anything for you," he says as he strides across the living room. "So, is there anything else we have to do before we leave?"

In fact, there is. I've been planning this surprise for months. And he hasn't made it easy. Now that he's living with me, I don't get much time to do anything behind his back.

Not that I do anything bad. But surprises are hard. And I find I'm a woman who likes to surprise her man.

Mostly with sexual escapades, but a surprise is a surprise, right?

"I just have to do one last sweep of my office, make sure I haven't forgotten anything, and then..." I shrug. "Who knows? I'm sure we'll find a way to kill time."

"How could you possibly have forgotten anything with the checklist Darcie made for you?"

He's not wrong. After we returned from MMM last year, and I filled her in on everything that happened, she's made a point to attend every signing since. And because she attends, she's made sure I'm more organized than ever.

"And part of that checklist is double-checking," I say with a laugh. "Be right back."

I race down the hall and into my office, closing the door behind me. Quickly stripping out of my clothes, I mentally run through my plan. I change into the black lace bra and thong set, and then pull on the thigh-high black leather boots I bought for just this occasion. Grabbing the gift bag of goodies on my way out, I return to the living room.

Lead is sitting on the couch, his back to the hallway, but he turns at the sound of my heels on the hardwood.

"Aw, fuck, Nova," he groans as he rises and walks toward me. "Turn around so I can get a good look at you."

I spin in a circle. The sound of his zipper reaches my ears, and I grin. When I'm facing him again, he has his cock out in his hand.

"Stunning."

I grab his free hand. "Come with me."

I drag him through the kitchen and out into the garage where he keeps his Harley. We've added and crossed off so many things on my never-ending checklist, but this is one I've kept to myself since my mom called and interrupted my explanation of the fantasy I had in the shower.

"What is going on?" he asks when I close and lock the door behind us.

We have time, but I'm not taking any chances in case Darcie arrives early. Bitch better not though.

"I'm gonna need you to strip," I tell him.

Lead is naked in record time. When he reaches for me, I back away.

"First, this." I thrust the bag at him.

He eyes me suspiciously, then the bag before taking it from me. He pulls out three boxes, which I've numbered so he knows what order to open them in. He tears into the first one, and grins.

"It's my latest book," I explain. "It's one I didn't tell you about."

"This is me," he says as he points to the cover.

"It is. I hope that's okay."

"It is." He closes the distance between us. "And the title? It's perfect."

"I thought *Forever Savage* fit. It's our story. I mean, it's fiction, of course, but it's based on us." I take the book from him and flip to the dedication page. "Read this," I say as I hand it back.

"This is for all the girls who don't believe in love. I'm here to tell you that it exists. The problem is it doesn't always present itself in fairy-tale form. Sometimes, if you're lucky, it's so much better than any bedtime story your mother ever read to you when you were a little girl."

So yeah, I believe in love now. But I mean what I wrote... it's not like I thought it would be. And I never would've found it if I hadn't opened myself up to the possibilities, to Lead.

"You make me believe, Lead," I tell him. "I still think fairy tales are shit, but love? It's real. With you, it's real. I love you so damn much I feel like I'll burst with it sometimes. It's not perfect, and it's not easy, but it is real."

"I love you too."

"I know."

Lead pulls me into his chest and kisses me. When I have to clench my thighs to keep from coming, I tug out of his hold.

"Open box two," I instruct.

"You're gonna be the death of me, Nova Stone," he growls.

"Yet, you love me."

"I do. More than life itself."

"Open box two," I repeat.

He hands me the book to hold while he opens the next box. Pulling out a bottle of lube and butt plug, he grins.

"These are new," he comments.

"They are," I confirm.

We crossed anal off the list months ago, and once again, he proved to me that something I write is also something I like. A lot.

I hand him the book and move to his Harley. Bending over the seat, I stick my ass in the air.

"Read page ninety-seven," I purr over my shoulder.

Lead scramble to open the book to the correct page, and his lips move as he silently reads. He flips the page, and then tosses the book to the floor and rushes toward me.

"Is this the scene you came up with last year at that motel?" he asks as he drags a fingertip through my ass crack.

"It is."

"Do I need box three?"

"Not yet."

Like the hero in my book, the hero he's become, Lead

puts the lube, butt plug, and his cock to work, acting out the scene in perfect detail. And I come three times.

When we're both spent, I say, "Now it's time for box three."

The remote-control vibrating panties in that box are put to good use over the next three days as we drive to Texas.

And on the way home a week later.

Motorcycles, Mobsters, and Mayhem author event proudly presents
The Mayhem Makers Series.
These standalone novels are brought to you by several bestselling authors specializing in writing twisted chaos. You'll get all the bikers, mobsters, and dark romance your heart can handle.

Follow us so you never miss a new release, as they can be added in at any time!

IF YOU LOVED FOREVER SAVAGE AND WANT TO READ THE BEGINNING OF LEAD'S RISE TO PRESIDENCY, CHECK OUT SOULLESS KINGS MC, WHERE HE FIRST APPEARS:

FENDER: BOOK #1

Fender...

One night. That's all it takes for a person's life to forever be changed. One chaotic, unexpected, inevitable night and hundreds of bullets, two of them hitting my parents. I was born to be a Soulless King, born with sworn enemies and a loyal streak. Like a phoenix, I rise from the ash and vow to bring hell upon those responsible.

The problem with my vow is I'm not sure who is to blame. They tell me it's the temptress with emerald eyes, the one who used to share my bed. How can I be sure since she left without giving me the chance to find out the truth?

Now that she's back, she won't get away before I ask my questions. But what if I don't like the answers?

Charlie...

As the princess of the Black Savages, I was raised to believe one thing: my club is my family, no matter what. But when they are responsible for shattering the life I created, I do the only thing I can. I run.

The thing about running is I can't do it forever. Life, past transgressions, tragedy... they hunt me down and drag me back, shoving me into the deep end of fate. And fate is a fickle bitch.

What if my fate is with *him*, the president of the Black Savages' sworn enemy?

PROLOGUE

They say your life flashes before your eyes at the moment just before death. They fucking lied.

Fender

Slick.

Wet.

Hot.

Perfect.

That's the only way to describe the pussy I'm buried in. Charlie moans and the sound seems to echo around us in flawless rhythm with the headboard banging against the wall.

"That's it, baby," I growl as I reach between our bodies and rub circles over her clit with my thumb.

Charlie's eyes resemble an emerald in its purest form, and I'm lost, drowning in a sea of green. They widen and her pupils dilate the second her orgasm begins. Tingles race down my spine, and my body tenses as I join her.

We explode together, and the sounds we've created die down. My heart is pounding, and her breathing is labored. I roll off of her, carrying her with me and tucking her into my side.

"Holy shit, Fender."

"What?" I ask, a grin tugging at my lips. She always says the same thing after we fuck. Always.

"It gets better every—"

"Fender, get the fuck out here!"

The pounding on my door and the urgency in Piston's voice has me springing from the bed and grabbing my gun from the nightstand. That's when it registers. Gunshots, yelling, glass shattering.

"Fender! Now!" Piston's fist is an inch away from my face when I throw open the door. "Black Savages stormed the club. Get dressed and c'mon!"

I glance over my shoulder and see Charlie shoving her legs into her jeans. Her ass is encased in the black lace I pulled off her body with my teeth not a half hour ago. I hate to see her cover her flesh, but I can't think about that right now.

"Get in the fuckin' closet and don't come out. Not for anything." I grip her bicep and drag her to the door in the corner of the room, throw it open and shove her in.

"Maybe I can talk to them. Maybe I—"

"No. They're past talking and so am I." I crush her lips in a bruising kiss before shutting the door in her face.

I dress as quickly as I can and mentally prepare for what I'm about to face. Certainly nothing good. I make my way down the hall, my gun cocked and ready to blow away any Savage that gets in my path.

I just pray it's not Dyno. It would be great to take out the president of the Black Savages, but I can't do that to Charlie. I can't kill her dad.

I round the corner into the main room of the clubhouse and am shocked at the carnage. The floor is littered with broken liquor bottles and booze. There's also blood and bodies, and it's hard to tell what club the deceased belong to.

"Fender!"

I whirl toward the voice and see my father, his shirt soaked in blood, kneeling on the floor. My mother is cocooned in his arms, her body limp. Everything else melts away. The shouting, the gunfire, the mayhem. Cold calm washes over me as I walk toward my parents, ignoring the bullets whizzing past my head. Maybe I'd get lucky, and one would take me out so I wouldn't have to face what I know is coming.

Time speeds up the closer I get. I drop to my knees. "Where are you hit?"

My father's stare is blank, empty. When he doesn't respond, I run my hands over his chest to determine if the blood is his or all from the hole I can now see in my mother's head. I don't allow myself to feel the loss. I can't afford to fall apart right now. My fingers hit a soft spot, a hole, on the left side of my father's chest. I rip the sleeves from his shirt and stuff the fabric in the hole to slow the bleeding. He hisses in pain, but that's his only reaction.

"Stay here," I shout at him, praying he hears what I'm saying. "I'll be back."

I lunge to my feet and storm into the middle of the room. I take a deep breath and find my first target. I point the gun and squeeze the trigger, not stopping until I've systematically taken out every Black Savage still standing, emptying the clip in the process.

"What the fuck was that?" Piston asks, walking through the bodies, kicking a few as he goes.

"Who'd we lose?" I survey the scene, trying to answer my own question.

"Stunner, Carbon, Phantom," Piston rubs his head, leaving a streak of blood. He's looking around, same as me. His head stops moving, and his gaze lands on something behind me. "Aw, fuck."

I slowly turn around, needing to see what he sees, and instantly regret it. My father is slumped over, both my parents dead. It's fitting, I suppose. They lived for the club and died for it. It's what they would've wanted, to go out together in a blaze of glory.

Bang!

I pivot around at the gunshot, shocked to hear it because I thought the chaos was over. Charlie's standing there, her eyes wide, her arms straight, the gun in her hand. I follow her gaze to the man she just killed. Sharp, the Black Savages' Sergeant at Arms, is lying on the floor with a bullet hole between his eyes.

"He was gonna kill you," she mumbles.

"You need to leave," Piston demands. "You don't belong here."

My eyes dart back and forth between the woman I love and my best friend. He's absolutely right. She shouldn't be here. Especially now. But I don't have it in me to make her leave.

"Did you do this?" Joker shouts from behind Piston, directing the question at Charlie. "Precious Black Savages' princess coordinates Soulless Kings' massacre. Isn't spreading your legs enough to secure your place?"

Charlie's arms drop to her sides, and the gun clanks to the floor. She's staring at me, silently begging me to defend her, protect her from the lies my brother's spewing. Problem is, I can't. What if he's right?

"Get the fuck out!" Joker shouts, pointing toward the exit.

Charlie's eyes well with tears as she turns and runs out the front door. In my twenty-three years on this Earth, I've stared down the barrel of a gun more times than I can count, and it doesn't hold a candle to what I'm experiencing right now.

I was born to be a Soulless King, raised to be a ruthless, loyal motherfucker. None of that prepared me for this moment. Nothing could make losing so much any easier to swallow.

They say your life flashes before your eyes at the moment just before death. They fucking lied.

Your life flashes before your eyes at the moment you lose everything you live for.

ABOUT THE AUTHOR

Andi Rhodes is an author whose passion is creating romance from chaos in all her books! She writes MC (motorcycle club) romance with a generous helping of suspense and doesn't shy away from the more difficult topics. Her books can be triggering for some so consider yourself warned. Andi also ensures each book ends with the couple getting their HEA! Most importantly, Andi is living her real life HEA with her husband and their boxers.

For access to release info and updates, be sure to visit Andi's website at www.andirhodes.com.

ALSO BY ANDI RHODES

Broken Rebel Brotherhood

Broken Souls

Broken Innocence

Broken Boundaries

Broken Rebel Brotherhood: Complete Series Box set

Broken Rebel Brotherhood: Next Generation

Broken Hearts

Broken Wings

Broken Mind

Bastards and Badges

Stark Revenge

Slade's Fall

Jett's Guard

Soulless Kings MC

Fender

Joker

Piston

Greaser

Riker

Trainwreck

Squirrel

Gibson

Flash

Royal

Satan's Legacy MC

Snow's Angel

Toga's Demons

Magic's Torment

Duck's Salvation

Dip's Flame

Devil's Handmaidens MC

Harlow's Gamble

Peppermint's Twist

Mama's Rules

Valhalla Rising MC

Viking

Mayhem Makers

Forever Savage

Saints Purgatory MC

Unholy Soul

Printed in Great Britain
by Amazon